Calling Off Christmas

Jeremy K. Brown

ISBN: 1466321261
ISBN-13: 978-1466321267

For my wife, Alli, who believes in me always.

And for my sons, William and James, who just believe.

CONTENTS

JEREMY K. BROWN

ACKNOWLEDGMENTS

Writing is purported to be a solitary pursuit, but the creation and completion of a book is most definitely a team effort. The members of my "team" that I would like to thank are: my wife, Alli, who is my most loyal fan and ardent critic. She is the audience of one for whom all my words are written. My boys, William and James, for keeping me young at heart and showing me every day how to be a better man. My mother, for always making the Christmas season such a special and wonderful time of year, and my sister for sharing with me all those joyous holidays and the days in between. To my in-laws, thanks for the love and support over the years, especially my mother-in-law. Thanks to my good friend Christopher Mari, one of the finest writers I have ever known, for the sharing of words, both in conversation and on the page. and to Vinnie Dacquino and all the members of the Mahopac Writer's Group for all the excellent advice and counsel. Thanks to Dana Chipkin for editing the manuscript and Margi Picciano for helping to format the book. Lastly, I would like to say a special thanks to my father, Kendall Brown, and my father-in-law, Peter Vincent, both of whom are loved and missed. I don't know if there's Christmas in Heaven, but if there is, I'd like to think that this book might find its way under their tree.

CHAPTER ONE

By now you know the whole story. Or at least you probably think you do. You've heard from people who were there, or people who say they were. But knowing the whole story and knowing the truth are two completely different matters. That's why I've decided to tell you my side of things. Of course, I still can't guarantee you that you'll know the truth when I'm done. Because, you see, my story's less about truth and more about faith.

It's probably best that we start with the introductions. I'm Jingles. Don't laugh, it's a family name. Besides, most people call me Jinn. If someone calls me by my full name, chances are they're either a stranger or I'm in some kind of trouble.

My relationship with the old man goes back a long way. And trust me when I say that you and I have very different perspectives on what the word "long" means. Let's just say we've been together forever and leave it at that. I'm what's known as a "walk-around guy." I keep tabs on his appointments, apprise him of new developments on both the Naughty and Nice lists, make sure he's up to date on weather patterns, which kids have moved, who still believes, who's on the fence. Basically, all the things he's too busy to keep up with himself. It's a tough job, but I like to think I do it well.

So, now that you know who I am, let me tell you my story. You'll want to hear it. It's the reason there's even a Christmas this year. In fact, if we're being totally honest, it's the reason you're holding this book in your hands. After all, not many people would be too keen on putting out a Christmas book when the holiday's been cancelled. And while most of these kinds of stories tend to kick off in the days leading up to Christmas, mine begins just as it's ending …

* * *

To the average person, Christmas Eve at the Pole must be a hubbub of activity, with everyone running around like lunatics making sure the day goes off without a hitch. And, truthfully, pretty much every other day of the year is like that around here. But on Christmas Eve it's a whole other story. See, that's the one night we elves have off. The toys have been made, presents wrapped, lists checked (sometimes twice) and the old man's out of the house. He leaves at dawn and doesn't return until the sun's creeping over the horizon on the 25th. And during that time we pretty much take it easy. After all, with 364 days of work under our belts, we're entitled to a little R&R. But not everyone has it that simple. The boys up in STC (that's Sleigh Traffic Control) are on their feet the whole livelong day. They're giving weather reports, flight patterns, and locations for commercial traffic. It's a constant stream of information that's being relayed to the Boss throughout the day and well into the night. Imagine Mission Control during any one of the moon landings and you'll have an idea of the organized chaos that unfolds every December 24th.

For the rest of us, though, the day is spent sleeping. Until, that is, right before he arrives back home. Now, I know most of you have never seen a sleigh landing, but let me do my best to take you there.

It all begins just before first light on Christmas. That's just about when the Boss passes over the Arctic Ocean, and the outer marker that lets the Tower know that he's on approach. At that moment, every elf is up and out of bed, peering out of windows or racing to whatever vantage point they can secure for themselves.

Up in STC, the atmosphere goes from pandemonium to a quiet, watchful state. All eyes and ears are on the team up in the air, making sure they touch down without a problem.

There's always one elf charged with direct communication with the old man, and his is pretty much the only constant voice you'll hear. Others will pipe up with information on downdrafts, wind eddies or rogue shears that might put him off course, but for the most part, it's just a one-on-one conversation between the Boss and SleighCom. On that night, I tuned in my radio to the STC band and listened excitedly as he talked the old man in.

"S-1, STC. We read you at the outer marker and have you on approach."

Santa's voice came over the speakers, crackling and faint as it traveled through the stormy atmosphere, but still unmistakably his. That soft, almost musical burr that can only come from one whose job is bringing joy to the faces of the world's children.

"STC, S-1, I've passed over Kaffeklubben. I'm reading you, but no visual yet."

Kaffeklubben Island is the closest landmass to us. Just off the Greenland Coast, the 1 km stretch of land is uninhabited and we've worked hard to keep it that way.

"Hold steady, S-1," replied SleighCom. "We're getting patches of fog. Might be a tricky landing this year."

"Could've used Rudy up here," came the gruff reply. Indeed, Rudolph was on the Disabled List this Christmas thanks to a wrenched knee at the 888th Reindeer Games.

"No worries, Boss. We've got you. Turn left 20 degrees on bearing 327 and hang tight."

"Roger that."

The back-and-forth exchange goes on like that for a while. Then, invariably, someone somewhere calls out "There he is! I see him!!!" And that's when it goes into overdrive.

"STC, S-1, I can't see a thing up here. The tarmac looks like one big blur."

"S-1, STC, we copy that," answered SleighCom. "We've got birds in the air to bring you in."

Although the team itself is comprised of only eight reindeer (whose names you no doubt know by now), there are still many other flying deer at The Pole that perform a variety of assignments. On this particular night, two were being sent up to guide the Boss back down to Earth. It's a pretty startling sight, watching these four-legged creatures pad their way out to the runway, looking ungainly and almost clumsy, and then take off with the grace and speed of an F-15. If you listen closely, you can hear the muffled *boom* when they hit Mach 1.

Now the elf monitoring the reindeer chimed in, relaying their position.

"STC, reading Caribou flight, they've got eyes on the Red Man."

"Caribou, STC, roger that. Eyes on the Red Man. Low and slow, take him down below the hard deck and bring him in. You're looking five-by-five."

At this point, he's usually in visual range, though this year was trickier without Rudolph's distinct red glow. Nevertheless, after a few moments of radio silence, the team dipped below the clouds and streaked its way down toward the ground, the unmistakable sound of bells jingling through the air.

Now the action shifts from the tower down to the tarmac. Instantly ground crews head out to greet the sleigh when it comes in. The escort deer veer off, giving the team a wide berth as they work their way lower and lower until at last, light as a feather, they hit the ground and gallop to a nice easy stop. At that point, there's about ten seconds of applause and everyone gets to work.

The first ones on the tarmac are the blanket crews. They race out to the deer and drape warm blankets over each of them, getting their body temperature back up after 24-plus hours above 30,000 feet. This is a special assignment and takes a rare breed of elf to do it. Reindeer are the pro athletes of our world and can be a bit temperamental when coming off of their biggest night. The only thing they want to see are hot blankets and hotter chocolate. Each deer is assigned a specific elf and that one elf is the only person who interacts with them at that moment. If you're at ground level, you'll hear each of their voices chatting their deer up.

"Great show, Blitzen, great show!"

"Any landing you can walk away from is a good one, Comet!"

"Where'd you learn that little kick when you took off, Dasher? Must've saved you at least 10 feet!"

Then after the reindeer have been warmed up, their harnesses are unclipped and they're taken to the stable for debriefing. The sleigh itself is quickly loaded onto a transport and driven to the hangar, where it's cleaned, serviced, and searched for lost presents or stowaway kids (shocking, but it happens). Beyond that, the Sleigh doesn't need much in the way of maintenance. It's pretty low-tech. I've tried to get the Boss to install a GPS or an onboard navigation system, but he refuses. He still likes to steer by the stars.

* * *

Once the team is back on the ground and everyone's been debriefed, the real party begins. The Christmas party that we hold up at the Pole no doubt rivals any bash you or any member of your family has ever thrown. If you don't believe me, you're certainly invited to the next one. Basically, it's 24 straight hours of feasting, dancing, and general merriment. It's the biggest day of the year here and the one time where no one has anything to worry about.

Usually, the boss kicks things off with his annual address, which is always a showstopper. Rumors abound that he employs speechwriters and punch-up guys to sweeten the words a bit, but I can assure you it's all off the cuff. I always look forward to hearing what he has to say, but this year something was off.

The band was in full swing by the time he made the scene. He came into the room and took the stage and everyone fell silent. All the ears in the room pricked up, waiting for the opening joke.

"Ummmm," he said, the echo of feedback framing his words.

As one, the room leaned in, eagerly anticipating the follow-up.

"Ummmm … thank you all for all your hard work this year."

Silence, broken only by a few awkward coughs. This was definitely not the usual speech.

"Every one of you put in a great effort … and … I'm sure next year will be even better, though let's not get ahead of ourselves. For now, it's back to business and if this should be our last Christmas together, well, it's been a good run, hasn't it?"

He put down the microphone, gave a cursory nod and strode off the stage. Everyone stood shocked a moment before some random reveler broke the stillness with a shout of, "Ladies and gentle-elves, the one and only Santa Claus!!!!" The rousing cry led to a wave of cheers and the celebration began anew. Amid all the merrymaking, only I stood there perplexed. For more than two thousand Christmases, this had never happened. Something was wrong, something serious enough to bring an end to Christmas altogether.

I contemplated following the old man, trying to get to the bottom of what was bugging him, but thought better of it. I'd known him a long time and knew when he needed some time for himself. His was a solitary life, in many ways, and there were times when he needed to take that in on his own.

So, I went back to the party, though the specter of his drawn and sad-looking face lingered in the back of my mind. By the time things had begun to wind down, I had strolled out onto the grounds to watch the morning creep its way over the ice. The band had packed it in and a few stragglers were singing "Silent Night" in passable form, considering the lateness of the hour. I sat on an outcropping of ice overlooking one of the larger glaciers that borders the property. The waning moon cast everything in blue, while a sliver of pink let me know that the new day was on its way.

As the singing rose into the lightening sky, I looked back at the house and saw one solitary light glowing softly in a second floor window. I could see Kris in silhouette staring out over the coming dawn. Though his face was obscured, his stooped posture and slumped shoulders made him look as though the weight of his years was finally bearing down on him. Seeing him there, forlorn and alone in the half-light, I was struck, for the first time in all the centuries I'd known him, by how very old he looked.

CHAPTER TWO

I didn't see much of the old man for the next few days. The Christmas fallout keeps me pretty busy and he and I usually don't sit down until sometime after the New Year. Whenever I did see him, though, he always had a faraway look in his eyes, like his mind was someplace entirely separate from where we were standing.

Finally it was a new year and I found myself late for our first meeting. It wasn't my fault. I was held up negotiating the reindeers' contracts for next Christmas. Yeesh. You would think that the prestige of being part of Santa's team would be enough, wouldn't you?

So now here I was, racing down the red-carpeted halls of the main house en route to his office. My stomach churned. One thing the Boss frowned upon was tardiness. After all, this was a guy who delivers presents to every single child on the planet in one night. All he expects from his employees is to be able to keep an appointment.

As I jogged along, my ears picked up the sound of muffled laughter coming from behind the door to one of the sitting rooms. Curious, I stopped in front of the door and pushed it open.

Walking into the room, I nearly broke my neck on some stray apples that were rolling around the floor like marbles. I looked up and saw a humongous cornucopia spilling fruits, pies, steaming Christmas goose and flaming puddings out onto the floor.

Seated at the hearth was a giant bearded man clad in a green robe with laurels of holly around his head.

"Ho, Ho!" he chortled, sounding like he'd just breathed in a heavy dose of laughing gas. "Come in, and know me better, man!!!!"

I shook my head. "C.P., I've spent over two hundred Christmases with you. I know you quite well, I think."

The Ghost of Christmas Present. A more joyful fellow you're not likely to meet, second only to the big guy himself, but his constant good cheer can get a bit tiresome at times. Especially when you have places you need to be. I gestured at him with my clipboard.

"Have this cleaned up before the Boss gets down here, before we both end up on the Naughty List. Permanently."

In response, the Spirit only laughed louder, slapping his knees and shaking the walls. My eyes rolled upward as I closed the door.

"Man," I muttered to myself. "Isn't *one* jolly fat man enough around here?"

Before I could contemplate my own question further, I ran smack into an amorphous black shape blocking the hallway and let out a scream.

"Yikes, Future! What have I told you about sneaking around the halls like that?"

The hooded figure didn't answer me, but merely gestured with his one visible hand.

"What?"

Again, the gnarled white hand silently pointed downward.

"What is it?"

No reply. The finger pointed on. Finally, I looked down at the shoulder bag that rested on my hip and realized what it was he wanted. I reached in and extracted a candy cane, placing it in his bony palm. The ghost nodded solemnly and floated on down the hall.

I hope none of you ever have a run-in with the Ghost of Christmas Future. Nice enough guy, but kind of a downer to be around. By his reckoning, every single

Christmas you spend from this one on will be fraught with misery, disaster, and outright doom. And they all involve washerwomen taking your bed sheets and selling them. I still don't know what *that's* all about, but I imagine a therapist would have a field day with it.

As you've probably guessed, every historical figure that has ever been associated with Christmas has found their way here. From Rudolph on down, they're all roaming the halls of the great house at any given time. Elves, bears, snowmen, even those mice that broke Mr. Trundle's Christmas clock all those years ago. The old man loves having them around, says it keeps the spirit of the season alive. That's fine for him, though; he doesn't have to put up with them day in and day out. Think it's easy? You try and have a civil discussion with the Heat Miser sometime.

Just then, my HollyBerry chirped.

"Hello?" I said. "Oh, hi, Mr. Grinch. Yes, your travel's all set. You land in Geneva day after tomorrow just in time for the convention. Sue should have your itinerary. Sure. OK, safe flight and we'll see you when you get back."

I slipped the phone in my pocket and laughed to myself. Forty years later, the world's cardiologists are *still* amazed at how someone's heart can grow three sizes in one day.

When I came into his office, the first sign that things weren't going to go well was the music. Or, more accurately, the lack thereof. The Boss *loves* Christmas music of all kinds. Whether it's "Deck the Halls" or John Denver's *Rocky Mountain Christmas* or Buster Poindexter singing "'Zat You, Santa Claus?" the old man has it all and plays it all. He loves the idea that people are writing songs about the holiday and about him. Not because of his ego or anything, but because it reminds him that the world still believes.

Today, though, I leaned against the door and heard … nothing. No music at all. *Uh oh*, I thought to myself. *Not a good sign.* Nevertheless, I had to go in. There was business to attend to. I pushed open the door, knocking as I came in.

"Morning, Boss."

He didn't turn around, still looking out at the snow that had begun to fall. "Come in, Jinn."

I took my seat across from his desk and opened up my notebook.

"Another banner year, don't you think?," I began. "Hundred-percent delivery rate, no stragglers and, best of all, no Naughty-Listers. No major offenders, anyway. All in all, one for the books."

He turned to face me and I looked into the eyes that had seen two thousand suns rise on two thousand Christmases.

"It was also my shortest delivery on record," he said.

"Well, yes," I agreed, "but we had a lot on our side. Favorable conditions, clear skies, and the deer were all in top shape. That Spinning class you signed them up for really … "

"Those weren't the reasons," he said with a wave of his hand. "Do you want to know why I had such a fast delivery this year?"

I knew enough to know this was a rhetorical question, so I simply zipped it and awaited the follow-up.

"Because I had next to no one to deliver to," he said. "Letters were at an all-time low this year. I checked down at the mailroom. They confirmed it for me."

Maybe I should tell you a little about how the letter system works here. Pretty much every child in the world at one time or another has written a letter to us. And those letters are confirmation of their belief in us and what we do here. As long as they send letters, we send gifts. Every letter sent is checked for authenticity, matched to a specific child, and placed in a file. This process goes on without a hitch until the first year that child does not send a letter. Immediately, their name is put on a watch list and the file is red-flagged for a possible case of "outgrowth." We usually give a pass the first year, sending out teams to observe the family, make sure the mailman didn't drop a letter or anything, but if the next Christmas season rolls around and still no letter, then their case file is closed and shredded. It happens, unfortunately, more often than I'd like. The

11

good news is, it doesn't have to. Believing in something wonderful shouldn't be something you grow out of. It should be something you hold on to, no matter how old you get. You see, the older you are, the harder life becomes. It helps to remember that there's still something wondrous happening in the world when the going gets too tough.

Can you do me a favor? If you're reading this right now, whether it's by yourself or with someone else, just let me know that you still believe, OK? It doesn't have to be anything major. Just say out loud, "I believe," and I'll hear you. Wherever you are, I'll hear you. And you'll actually be doing me a favor as well, because the more people believe, the better things run up here. More on that later.

I shifted in my seat. "Well, times are hard, that's true. Kids are growing up faster."

"It's not only that," he said. "They're not even interested in what we produce here anymore. No one wants toys. They all want video games, iPods, cell phones. Eight years old and they're asking me for a cell phone!"

"It's been that way for a while," I said with a nod. "But our contracts with Apple, Nintendo, and all the major electronics companies are still standing. They make 'em, we ship 'em. The world changes, we adjust."

He laughed a quiet chuckle, sardonic with a hint of resignation. "Boxing up PlayStations on Christmas Eve. Is that what it's come to? We used to make magic up here, remember?"

I shrugged. "Kris, I've been with you from the beginning. From the days when you were just a peddler going from village to village. We built all of this up from nothing. But we have to accept that the world we started in just doesn't exist anymore. You can't go around putting oranges in socks hung by the fireplace these days. Heck, a lot of kids don't even have fireplaces. We had to work out that deal with MasterLock, remember?"

Just so you know, every house built that doesn't have a fireplace comes installed with a special type of lock that only Santa can open. The parents leave the key out for the Boss on Christmas Eve and he comes right in. Simple. And, in my opinion, the way to go. We'd save a lot on laundry bills, for one thing.

"I know," he said with a sigh. "Deals are our stock and trade now, I suppose. Buying ourselves more time just to stay in business another Christmas."

I could see there was no shaking him out of this, so I opted just to placate him for the time being. Looking back, I wish I had listened longer. It would have saved me a lot of headaches down the road. But right then, I had things to discuss.

"Look, Kris, it'll all be okay," I said in an attempt to console him. "The world's always going to need a Santa Claus."

He smiled, a forced one, but it was progress. "I know, Jinn, I know."

"Now, let's get business out of the way," I said. "That guy from Vermont called again. Claims he's got some organic reindeer food that'll ensure a glossier coat and faster flight times. I told him we'd look into it."

Kris nodded. "Have him send samples in time for the Reindeer Games this summer."

"You bet," I said, checking it off the docket. "NORAD wants your flight patterns for next Christmas before Memorial Day in order to give them time to prepare."

Yes, every government agency in the world knows about us. It's the only way we could stay in business, especially these days. Here's the way it works: Sometime around the end of the First World War, when the planet really began to get smaller, a dialogue was opened between us and a few highly-placed government officials. We brought them up here, showed them around, and struck an agreement: We'd stay out of their way, they'd stay out of ours. Only a few people actually know the details, mind you. The "Redbird File," as it's known, is classified Above Top Secret. Probably more people know the truth about aliens than they do about everything that happens up here. Not that I'm confirming anything about aliens, mind you. That's someone else's book to write.

So that's the deal. And, for the most part, it's worked out just fine. Of course, there was that slight slip-up in 1968. On Christmas Eve of that year, as Apollo 8 circled the Moon, Frank Borman announced, "Please be advised, there is a Santa Claus." It happened. Look it up for yourselves. Most people laughed it off as a clever one-liner, but I can assure you there were a few people well above Col. Borman's pay grade who went white as sheets in that instant. It didn't matter much to us, though. No one in the real world gave it much thought, and if anything, it was a bit of free publicity.

On and on it's gone. Every year, we keep all those in the know well-informed as to our comings and goings. It wouldn't do to be shot down over Nevada one year because someone at Nellis Air Force Base mistook us for an incoming MiG.

The Boss scanned the flight plan STC had drawn up for him. It was just a prelim, of course, but we start on these things early. Hey, if you were planning a one-night flight around the world, stopping at every house along the way, wouldn't you like to have your itinerary in order?

He pushed it across the table to me. "Looks good for now. Keep me posted."

"Will do."

I got up to leave and, as I reached the door, one last thing occurred to me.

"Oh," I said, snapping my fingers. "The EPA's got a new guy they want to send up."

"What about Sinclair?"

Remy Sinclair had been our guy at the Environmental Protection Agency for years. When you have an operation this big running smack-dab on a heap of floating pack ice, you need to make sure you've got friends in green places. He was a crazy old hippie who just loved the fact that he was clued in on Santa and the happenings up here. Great guy. We even had his whole family up for Christmas Eve a few times. A slight breach of protocol, sure, but that's how much we loved him. He hung up his spurs after last year and moved to Seattle. Bainbridge Island, I think. I've got his Christmas card on my fridge.

"Retired."

He sat back in his chair and whistled softly. "Remy retired, huh? Boy, we are getting old."

"Don't worry about it, Boss," I said. "We'll take this new guy through the program and bring him up to speed. Totally routine."

Totally routine. In all my years of employment, I have said only a few things that I've come to regret. That was one of them.

CHAPTER THREE

The next few weeks sailed by in a flurry of phone calls, meetings and general insanity. Before I knew it, it was getting close to spring and I found myself standing on the helipad outside the main house watching the EPA copter descend from a bright blue polar sky.

The craft touched down and its side door slid open. Out stepped a nervous-looking man with thinning brown hair and pale, mottled skin. Tyler Maddox, Remy's replacement. He was dressed in an expensive-looking suit, over which was draped an equally-expensive tan topcoat that flowed down to his heels and flared up in the windstorm kicked up by the rotors. He shielded his eyes with a leather-gloved hand and looked over at me.

"Are you…" he opened his Day Planner and flipped through it, a process that took him longer than usual as the wind continually blew the pages back as fast as he could turn them. "Are you Jingles?"

I shook his hand. "Jinn," I said. "Everyone just calls me Jinn. Welcome to the North Pole, Mr. Maddox."

"Thank you," he said. Clipped. All business.

"Very well, then," I said with a nod. "Let's get inside and I can show you around."

He looked up at the main house, a three-story Victorian mansion rising up tall and majestic from the ice sheet, its many turrets rising above the roof lines as candles shone in dormer windows. Off in the distance, a few reindeer flew overhead on patrol as elves bustled in and out of the factory, readying the day's workloads. A few of the younger ones skittered about on the ice, kicking frozen chunks back and forth, laughing gaily. Maddox stood a moment, completely dumbstruck at the scene before him. The boardroom veneer melted away for just a second. And in that second, he looked like a man who was fighting against everything his senses were telling him.

"Trust me, Mr. Maddox," I said with a grin. "We know."

Once inside, I took him up to my office, where a tray of hot chocolate and Pfeffernüsse was waiting for us. If you've never had Pfeffernüsse, then please do me a favor. Put this book down, run to your nearest market, and pick up a box. You'll thank me and I think it will enhance your enjoyment of this story. Please. Go now. It's okay. I'll wait.

Ready? Good. Now, as I was saying, Maddox and I sat down in my office and talked over business. I won't say I disliked the guy, but I got an uneasy feeling from him. He struck me as having been one of those kids who just didn't quite believe from the start. I made a mental note to check with Kid Resources to see when his file had been shredded. Also, for the head of the EPA, he didn't seem overly … environmentally minded. Something about his clothes, his demeanor just didn't wash. Remy was one of those guys who was really in tune with everything around him. He got it, all of it. This guy? Well, he looked as though the Earth were another piece of business to him. Something else to be checked off in the ledger.

"So," he said. "You live up here year 'round?

"Never anywhere else," I said.

"Cost of living must be a bear, huh?" he said. "Everything flown in and so on?"

"No, we're entirely self-sufficient," I said. "Everything here is made on the premises."

17

"How?" he said with an incredulous tone. "How could you grow anything up here? No soil, no water, no livestock."

I looked at him, knowing the answer, but unsure as to how he was going to take it. "Magic," I said.

His face turned to a mask of disbelief. "Magic?" he said, though it wasn't the question he was really asking. The real question was: what kind of a fool do you take me for?

"That's right," I said. "Look, there's obviously a practical side to what goes on up here, you know that. But a lot of what we do, the flying reindeer, delivering gifts in one night, a fat man who squeezes down chimneys, a lot of it hinges, well ... on magic."

I could he wasn't sold, so I pressed on. "Take the presents, for example," I said. "Every Christmas, we deliver millions of packages around the world. The biggest FedEx truck in the world couldn't hold them all, and we deliver them in a sleigh! So, using a little magic, we shrink everything down so that all the packages, from action figures to plasma TVs, are the size of jewelry boxes. Then, at each house, the old man resizes the presents and delivers them. Voila!"

"I see," he said. Instantly he popped open his planner, unscrewed his Mont Blanc pen and, from what I could tell, wrote the word "Magic" on the page, followed by a large question mark.

He snapped the book shut. "Well, are you going to give me the grand tour?"

"Absolutely," I said. "And trust me, if you're not a believer in magic, chances are you will be when we're done."

* * *

It was a crystal clear morning, so I opted to take one of the ground sleighs out. Some people prefer taking the tram, which we had installed here about ten years ago, but to me it spoils a lot of the fun. For all you know, you could be taking the train in any major city instead of traveling through a place that, until now, existed only in your dreams. Whenever we get visitors and weather permitting, I always take them by sleigh.

We got underway and began skimming along the tundra. The sky was bright blue, and illuminated the snow and ice, making everything look as though it were glowing. The buildings on the compound stood out against the landscape like decorations on a never-ending birthday cake. As we traveled, I could see how uncomfortable Maddox was in the cold. His face was red and blotchy and his body contorted in a bizarre dance as it struggled to find warmth. I tossed him a blanket from under my seat.

"Try this," I said. "The Boss uses them all the time."

Maddox wrapped the blanket around himself and instantly seemed to warm up. His face brightened.

"Electric?" he asked.

"No, it's ..."

"Don't tell me," said Maddox, "Magic."

I shrugged. What did he want me to do, apologize for the way we ran things up here?

"You really believe in that stuff?" he went on.

"It's not so hard to believe in, really?" I said. "It's been a part of our lives from the beginning. Yours, too."

"I believe in what I can see," Maddox scoffed.

"It's that simple, is it?" I said. "Let me ask you something. Do you drive a car?"

"Of course," he said. "Mercedes SL."

"And do you know exactly how it works. Every part, I mean? How the internal combustion engine makes the car move, how the transmission shifts to accommodate changes in speed, how your GPS knows exactly where your house is?"

"Well ... no, not precisely," he said.

"And yet that doesn't keep you from getting behind the wheel every morning, does it? You just trust in the fact that what you don't know, what you don't see, will still get you to where you're going safely."

Maddox nodded. "You make a convincing argument," he conceded. He looked out at the world rushing past. "And this magic, it powers the whole place?"

"Not entirely," I said. "We still rely on conventional means of power as well. Mostly steam turbines powered from the water under the ice."

"How much power are we talking about?"

"That would be a question for our energy division," I said. "They're the ones keeping us running. Your predecessor put the program in place."

"Hmmmm," said Maddox, scrolling through his notes. "And there's been no increase in emissions over the years?"

"None that I'm aware of," I said, suddenly picking up on where he was going with this line of questioning. "You're not looking to shut us down, are you?"

Maddox smirked. "Well, not without probable *Claus*," he said, and his smirk shattered in a gale of laughter that sounded almost canned. I looked at him askance.

"My secretary," he said, almost apologetically. "She thought it would make a good icebreaker."

"Points for effort," I said, cracking a smile. "Shall we keep the tour going?"

* * *

Our first stop was the Observatory. This is where all the kids in the world are monitored day in and day out. Want to know how he sees you when you're sleeping? Here's your answer. Of course, the Boss doesn't do all the work himself. It's too time consuming. There's a whole team of observers who keep watch using any of the thousands of telescopes that peer out onto the four corners of the world. For some of the harder-to-reach places, we have a couple of listening dishes on loan from NASA.

It's a tough job, observing. You have to be skilled at reading behavior patterns, provocation for naughtiness, shifts in mood, environmental concerns. It requires years of schooling and on-the-job training. I considered it for a time but found I didn't have the discipline.

We entered the observatory and walked up a spiral staircase to the scopes. Along the way, I explained the process a bit, though I can't be certain whether Maddox heard anything I was saying or not. He didn't seem all that interested.

At the top of the stairs, Maddox took in the sight of the enormous domed room with its cavernous ceiling and endless array of scopes jutting out into the sun-struck morning sky. The walls were laced with a lavish network of catwalks, over which scurried hundred of observers, each jotting notes and sending memos through vacuum tubes to the boss's office. He looked around.

"Impressive," he said. "And you have your eyes on every child in the world?"

"Pretty much," I said with a nod. "Obviously we take into account factors of religion and overall belief, but otherwise, we're watching."

"And the parents are okay with all of this?"

"Very much so," I said. "In fact, most parents are grateful for our help. Kids are better behaved during the Christmas season than any other time of year."

As an aside, I should probably tell you that, yes, parents also know we exist. We maintain an arm's-length relationship with every mom and dad out there. When their first child is born, a letter is sent from the Pole to the new parents. If they respond, the lines of communication are open. Contact is kept strictly through the mail, and the occasional mall Santa who's helping us out. We find it's a great way to ensure that kids get what they want (the right presents), and parents get what they want (peace and quiet).

Maddox looked at me, curious. "And what about coal? Is there any truth to that rumor?"

"We tried it in the early years," I admitted, "but it caused more problems than it solved. These days, we find the threat works much better than the actual application."

"So even the naughty kids get gifts?"

"It's not quite that black and white," I said. "But if you're worried about yourself, don't be. We'll take care of you."

* * *

After the Observatory, we hit the Present Pavilion, where all the toys are boxed, wrapped, and prepped for shipment. As we get closer to the big day, this place is a maelstrom of activity, with machines pumping and rattling in rhythm, elves buzzing about the floor shouting orders, and the air crackling with the sound of wrapping paper being ripped, torn, folded and taped. On this day, though, it was still early in the season, so it was just the skeleton crew on deck. The floor was still busy enough to look impressive to an outsider, mind you. Packages rattled along the conveyer belts, bouncing slightly as they passed over the endless rollers, machines spit out paper from various dispensers, colored, patterned, themed, cutting them off at their desired length with a steady, definitive *ka-chunk*. Along the conveyer route, lined up like military cadets, stood the wrappers themselves. The Boss has always insisted that every gift be hand-wrapped, just like the old days. You'd think that would be the least-desired job at the Pole, but that's where you'd be mistaken. Wrapping gifts is a big honor up here. Think about it: the next person who holds that gift will be a child on Christmas morning. Some elves take years to study and master the artistry of wrapping, and many of them put their own distinctive signatures on their work. If you ever get a gift wrapped in bright red paper, look for a small black "P" embossed underneath, right-hand corner. That's my cousin Peg, one of the top wrappers on the floor.

Peg wasn't there today. Today it was mostly older elves trying to keep busy. The big-ticket items usually didn't roll in until closer to Thanksgiving, but the crew was keeping busy wrapping what we call the boilerplates, generic gifts that are usually used to fill out a standard house visit: baseball bats, footballs, dolls, that sort of thing. It was always good to have a surplus in case you suddenly come up short.

"Do any gifts ever get lost or sent to the wrong people?" Maddox asked.

"Not often," I said, "but it's been known to happen from time to time. You're not still upset about that pink terrycloth bathrobe you got in 1989, are you?"

"How … "? he asked, and I simply tapped my head in reply. By the look on his face I sensed that he might be warming up to the idea of magic after all. Unfortunately, as I soon learned, it wasn't enough.

CHAPTER FOUR

After the tour was over, we made our way back to the Boss's office. Once we arrived, we sat down in a couple of red overstuffed chairs and waited. I was nervous; my senses hummed like bass strings plucked by phantom hands. Something about Maddox just didn't sit right with me. This feeling was exacerbated after taking him through the power plant. Seeing his face as he watched the giant steam turbines turn, drawing the water up from beneath the ice sheet, I could sense his concern. His lips thinned out until they were almost invisible and his pen worked furiously, scribbling down notes in a rapid style that was almost like automatic writing.

Now we sat silently in Kris's office, Maddox tapping away on his iPad, me tapping the arm of the chair and glancing around. The ticking of the grandfather clock had grown so loud it sounded as though someone was knocking repeatedly on the door. Finally the Boss strode in, shook hands all around, and then took a seat. Maddox wasted no time getting right down to it.

"Look," he said. "It's obvious you run an impressive facility here, but I've got to tell you, something's off."

"Meaning?" I asked

"Meaning that in the past year we've seen about 80 cubic miles of the polar ice sheet disappear. At the rate we're going, that number is likely to double."

"Are you blaming us for this?" asked Kris.

"Not directly. But you can't deny that your operation here could be a factor. The energy output of this place is staggering, and I for one am not convinced about its environmental viability."

"Can we talk plainly, then?" I asked. "What are you suggesting?"

Maddox leaned forward, his hands folded. "I'm suggesting that we shut down this facility until we can determine whether or not you are directly affecting the climate changes in this hemisphere."

I nearly fell out of my chair. Shut down the North Pole? Shut down Santa's Workshop? He couldn't be serious. No one could mean such a thing. Obviously Maddox sensed my disbelief, because he plunged ahead.

"I'm very serious, Mr. Jinn," he said. "And though I don't like it any more than you do, I have to do what I think is in the best interests of the agency."

"The agency?" I said, barely able to speak at this point. "What about the world? You shut us down and you might as well cancel Christmas!"

Maddox and I fell into a heated exchange at this point that does not bear repeating. In fact, I only bring it up because the two words that finally ended the debate came from the Boss and forever changed our lives.

"How long?"

"Sorry?" Maddox said.

"How long would you need to shut us down for?"

Quickly, Maddox sifted through his papers, then tapped out some numbers on his iPad. "Five, maybe six months," he said at last.

That settled it, in my mind. The discussion was over, this guy could return to whatever glass-and-steel bureaucratic palace he'd ridden out from and we could get back to business up here. I was relieved, glad that this was all behind us. I looked at the boss, hoping to see some of the same relief in his eyes. Instead, I saw something else entirely.

"Do it," Kris said.

I stared at him, unsure of what I'd just heard. "Excuse me?" I asked.

"Do it," he said. "Close down the factory. Make the necessary preparations and shut everything down."

Maddox, as stunned as I was over this turn of events, opted not to argue any further. Instead, he gathered up his things and prepared to scurry out, content with his victory.

"Thank you for your time," he said. "I'll file my report and we'll get an evaluation team out here immediately to go over this place point by point. We'll have you back up and running in no time."

With that, he was gone in a rustle of paper and the *click-clack* of expensive footwear. The silence that followed his departure was deafening. It was a hollow expanse of stillness that spoke volumes. At last, the old man spoke up.

"Don't be so dramatic, Jinn," he said gruffly, as he went back to work.

"The irony of your saying that to me is truly astounding," I replied. "Considering you've just made the most disastrous decision in the history of this operation!"

He gazed at me through tiny spectacles perched on his bulbous nose. Even in the midst of what could be our very downfall, I detected the faint curl of a grin beneath his beard.

"Maybe a dramatic decision is precisely what we need around here," he said.

"What we need around here is a dose of common sense!" I argued. "Not a knee-jerk reaction to an off-the-cuff suggestion. I mean, have you considered the magnitude of what you've done, here? What it will do to us?"

"Since you seem so convinced that I have not," Kris said, "why don't you illuminate me?"

"It's April," I said. "That leaves us seven months to get ready. Eight, if we push it. And with our operations closed down for six of those, that leaves us two months to receive lists, parcel out gifts, package them and prep them for delivery. To say nothing

26

about what this will do for our observation for the year. It will be impossible to get an accurate assessment of behavior in that amount of time!"

"Don't worry," the old man said, "I've got it covered."

"Oh, really," I said, sitting back and folding my arms. "This ought to be good."

"First, we contact every manufacturer with whom we do business, let the top brass there know what's happening and ask that they keep it quiet. Then we split the workforce up. We divide everyone into teams and send them out to every factory out there, put them on staff and have them speed up productivity."

"And then what?" I asked. "They'll use the factories to make gifts?"

"Most of them do it already," he answered. "We'll have a percentage of each factory's output go directly to us with our operation covering the cost. We've got more than enough saved up so that won't be a problem."

"And observation?"

"Send teams out into the field," Kris said. "Do it the old-fashioned way, going from house to house, listening to conversations, talking with teachers, ferreting out whatever info they can on the sly."

"That's going to be tough in this day and age," I said.

"These guys are pros," the Boss said with a wave of his hand. "They'll blend in."

He sounded confident. I was willing to give him that. But this was a plan in which a million things could go wrong, and probably would. However rosy a picture he painted, I smelled catastrophe nonetheless.

"And the kids?" I pressed on. "How will they get their letters to you?"

"Simple," he replied. "We'll forward them to my new address."

"Your new address?" I asked. "I thought they were shutting down the factories, not the residences."

"That may be," said Kris, "but I think this is a good time for me to get out and stretch my legs a bit. I've been living here for what … two thousand years? Maybe it's time to try something different."

"Where will you go, then?" I asked.

"I've got a friend in New York who owes me a favor," Kris said. "Something about a Radio Flyer wagon back in '71. "He's got a farm upstate that he never uses. It's big, quiet, isolated. The perfect spot. I'll even bring the deer with me. They'll love it."

"Does this place have a phone?"

"I would assume so," the old man shrugged. "Why?"

"Well," I said. "I'll need to stay in touch with you somehow, won't I?"

At this, Kris laughed, the classic laugh that has been written about in stories and songs for generations. It was the first time I'd heard it since before last Christmas and, in spite of the approaching disaster, it felt pretty darn good to hear again. Until, that is, I heard what came next.

"Why, Jinn," he said, still laughing heartily. "Didn't I tell you? You're coming with me!"

CHAPTER FIVE

Did I say that disaster was approaching? Well, that was one of many things I was wrong about. The moment I left the Boss's office, I knew that disaster was not approaching. It was already here; having landed right in the center of our cozy little lives with a big wet *splat*.

Immediately after our meeting I had to set about closing down an operation that had run undisturbed and without ceasing for two straight millennia. Most people have a hard time putting their life on hold to go on vacation for two weeks. What I was planning had consequences that could ruin the Christmases of nearly every person on the planet.

The first thing I did was call everyone together to make the announcement. There was some grumbling, that was to be expected, but for the most part, everyone took it rather well. Truthfully, I think they were just too stunned by the news to make much of a fuss about it.

After that came a meeting with the local engineers, whose families first built the Pole brick by brick. They'd kept it running ever since, upgrading equipment, making sure everything ran smoothly. And now here I was, asking that they switch it all off. It's not as easy as pulling a lever and grinding everything to a stop. Shutting down the operation, as it turned out, would require a very precise undertaking that would ensure that nothing was damaged and, when this whole mess was over, that it could all be powered back up again without any trouble. I told the engineers that I wanted a power-down/power-up plan on my desk by tomorrow morning and then left with every one of them wondering just how on Earth they were going to pull it off.

On and on it went, meeting with the observers, calling the CEOs of every toy, electronic, gadget and game company on the globe and filling them in, breaking the news to the reindeer. A never-ending succession of phone-calls made and received, e-mails sent and replied to, tears shed, angry mutterings made, and suggestions voiced that the old man had lost his mind. I answered every complaint and soothed every fear, all the while wondering if, when all was said and done, they were absolutely right.

Finally, the last day came just as the summer was about to arrive. I loved summer at the North Pole. The sun rides high in the sky, turning the ice sheets blue and shimmering, the temperature sits at just above freezing. Christmas is on the horizon, but still far enough away that time slows down a bit. It's a freewheeling, easy season and it killed me that I was going to miss it. But we all answer to somebody, and right now my boss was walking alongside me through an empty house, going through the final checklist.

"OK," he said. "All of the factory personnel have been moved offsite, correct?"

"That's right," I answered. "They're entrenched in their respective assignments and we should expect to start seeing product within a month."

"Perfect. And the observers?"

"Same deal. I've been in touch with local law enforcement so they're aware of what's going on. It wouldn't do to have a rash of APBs on tiny people peeking in windows and making notes. We're working in tandem with the individual municipalities to make sure everything's on the level."

"Excellent, excellent," Kris said. "What about the property itself?"

"Engineers are standing by," I told him. "They'll wait for our dust-off and once we're airborne they'll cut the power. A skeleton crew will stay behind to work with the EPA's eval team and prep the place for power-up when we return."

"Great," said Kris. "And how are we getting out of here?"

We reached the tarmac at that moment and Kris had his answer. I'd taken the sleigh out and polished it up for its somewhat premature flight. The deer were hitched up and waiting, huffing slightly and pawing at the ground.

"I figured if we're going to leave, why not at least go in style?"

The Boss smiled. "There's a reason you're my number-one guy, Jinn."

"Several, in fact," I said. "Now, I've made arrangements for all mail to be forwarded to our new address in New York, but we won't start seeing letters until around Thanksgiving, so that's not an immediate concern."

Kris nodded. "Thanksgiving," he said. "That reminds me, have we been in touch with Macy's?"

"Already done," I said. "In fact, it's going to work out well being closer to the city this year. Relatively, speaking, of course."

"Well, then," he said, "I guess there's nothing else to worry about then, is there?"

"Just the flight south."

Kris sighed and looked around one last time, taking in the place that had been his home since a time well before people had even known the world was round.

"It's hard," he said quietly, "leaving like this. Harder than I would have thought."

"It's only temporary," I said, trying to convince myself as much as him. As collected as I might have sounded, inside I was fighting panic at the lunacy of what we were about to do.

"Of course," he said and shook himself from his reverie. "Then let's get moving."

He climbed into the sleigh just as cool and confident as he is every twenty-fourth of December and with a snap of the reigns we got underway.

The deer trotted up to speed and then began to run faster and faster. The ice beneath our skids slid by with a hissing that sounded like steam escaping a boiler. It was then that I realized that in all the years I'd worked at the Pole, this was my very first takeoff.

Now it seemed as though we were moving at light speed. The ice was a white blur, the stars in the night sky streaking past like meteors. The sleigh jostled and bumped, making me feel as though I would at any moment be tossed to the ground and shatter like glass. All the while, the boss held the reins confidently, with the airy looseness that comes only with experience. He controlled the deer with subtle, effortless wrist motions, speeding them up or slowing them down with just the faintest tug or flick.

Just then, I saw Donner rear up and leave the ground. The other deer soon followed suit, curving upwards into the night with the precision of a military unit. As they became airborne, the sleigh was pulled up along with them. It felt as though an invisible hand had reached down and plucked us from the ground. Instinctively, I peered over the side to watch the ice sheet retreat behind me. I fully expected to be gripped by sudden and violent vertigo, but instead all I felt was euphoria. The sky was velvet blue, dimpled with stars. Beyond our home on the ice, I could see the sea stretching out endlessly, a rolling, foamy blanket of grey and white. My brain only vaguely comprehended that I was seeing these things in this way for the first time. I was filled with an inexplicable joy to be up here, riding the wind, powered only by eight reindeer. It was a potent reminder of the magic that fueled our lives here.

But then I saw a sight that extinguished my elation the way a pair of pinched fingers snuffs out a candle's flame. Far below us I saw our home at the Pole, blazing bright for one last glorious second before the power was cut, plunging it into blackness and banishing it from my sight.

CALLING OFF CHRISTMAS

CHAPTER SIX

The flight to New York was pretty uneventful, apart from a couple of stomach-lurching maneuvers while avoiding passing 747s. I even managed to sleep part of the way. It was only when I began to feel a sudden change in temperature that I stirred and realized that we had left the confines of our frozen paradise completely behind and were now in the grip of summertime in the lower 48.

I had never felt heat outside before, at least heat that wasn't generated by a fire or some other artificial source. It was a thoroughly unpleasant sensation, like sitting in a hot steam room and being covered with a horse blanket. People lived like this? And not only that, they enjoyed it? I hung my head over the railing, grateful for the wind whipping past and the cooling effect it gave.

At last, we began to descend as we reached our final destination. And it was here that the problems began. As you know, reindeer are experts at landing on roofs. They can touch down in the middle of a sleet storm with zero visibility and a sheet of ice an inch thick covering the shingles. But there's one fundamental difference between a winter landing and a summer landing: trees. You see, the entire landing area was obscured. Now, I had said that they should aim for a clearing and set down there, but no. They felt like showing off and decided to fly straight for the roof, despite the fact that all they could see were leafy bushels and jutting branches.

We came in hard and instantly Donner realized we'd overshot the mark. As a result, rather than circle around for another pass, he simply set down on the barn across from the main house. Branches smacked us in the face, leaves were torn off and fluttered about in the air, birds and other assorted tree-dwelling creatures were scared from their homes and now scurried about the sleigh in bewilderment.

Finally, we came to a short, abrupt halt on the roof of the barn. I performed a cursory exam to make sure I hadn't lost anything vital to my survival in the landing and took a deep breath, about to give the deer the tongue lashing of a lifetime.

That's when the roof gave in.

One sleigh, an elf, a jolly fat man, and eight not-so-tiny reindeer came crashing through the barn roof in a cloud of dust, splinters, and hay. It was a miracle no one was hurt. After lying there stunned, we all struggled to our feet and took stock of our situation. Thankfully, everyone survived the fall with little or no injury. A reindeer with a broken leg is the last thing we needed. Not only would it be impossible to train a replacement under these circumstances, but they're also just plain ornery to be around. The sleigh, however, was a different story. It was smashed. Probably irreparably. This was a more serious issue.

I had a backup sleigh arriving with a cadre of elves to run day-to-day operations at the house. But this one was a smaller model, good for quick runs and recon flights. For Christmas Eve, we were going to need the big guns, and unless we could find something that could handle an around-the-world flight, the Boss wasn't going anywhere. One more crisis to solve. I made a mental note to start calling trustworthy craftsmen and I reminded myself to get that roof repaired. This is where the deer would be staying and I know how they can be when the living arrangements aren't five-star.

And yet, just as our situation looked grimmer than ever, there was Kris, dusting himself off and chortling under his breath. He looked around, his eyes dancing slightly, then he spread his arms wide.

"Welcome home!"

* * *

Now, I don't want you to think I'm a spoiled elf based on what I'm about to say, but you have to understand, when you live at the North Pole, anything else is going to be a bit of a comedown. But what we ended up with was a bit more than a comedown. It was a hard fall to Earth.

The house was an eighteenth-century farmhouse that sat isolated on thirty acres. It was private, so it had that going for it. But when I say "eighteenth century," I don't only mean when it was built. I also mean the last time it was maintained. To call this place dilapidated would be an insult to dilapidated homes everywhere. It sagged under its own weight, perhaps a sneeze away from total collapse. It swayed and moaned in the summer wind, calling to mind an old woman in extreme discomfort. The porch was a death trap, with only about a third of its planks still intact. The front door, such as it was, hung by a thread and slammed repeatedly against the doorframe.

"Gee, Boss," I said. "What did you give this guy, socks?"

"What do you mean?" he asked.

"Well, you had to do something to make him angry enough to send us here."

He chuckled slightly. "It's not that bad. We'll fix it up ourselves, turn it into someplace really special."

"I'd just be happy if it didn't fall around our ears."

The door groaned open, sounding like every haunted house cliché you've ever imagined, and then fell off its hinges. A cloud of dust rose up where it landed. By this point, I was past making comments and merely shook my head.

Gingerly, we made our way up the creaking stairs. I silently thanked God that I was born an elf, while at the same time taking note of the Boss's girth and hoping that the ancient wood could handle the strain.

When we reached the upstairs hall, I saw a chandelier hanging over the stairwell, its baubles chiming slightly as it swayed in the slight breeze. I reached out and flicked the switch to turn on the lights. Instantly there was a buzzing, followed by a pop as every bulb in the chandelier burst. At that moment, there was a flurry of black as a group of sleeping bats was startled from inside the light fixture. They swirled around angrily before finding an open window and chittering away into the night.

In the wake of this display, I simply stood mute. Was this all a joke? Some kind of cosmic prank? Or was it a punishment of some sort? I looked at Kris and saw that same grin.

"At least we'll have company," he said.

That's when I lost it. I tossed my bag down and looked him square in the eye.

"This is all a game to you, isn't it?"

"Jinn…"

"No, that's it," I went on. "This has got to be a game. Either that or you've gone completely insane."

His face changed. "I'd be careful with your words."

"Like you were with your actions?"

"What precisely do you mean by that?" he asked.

"I think you know," I retorted. "You didn't give a second's thought to leaving behind everything we'd built up there. To uprooting thousands of people who'd stood by you since the beginning."

"Did it ever occur to you that I didn't have a choice?"

"You're wrong," I said, fury now choosing my words for me. "You've always had a choice in everything that's ever happened at the Pole. It's us who were left without a choice. All of us who were scattered around the country because of some silly notion that you had."

"Silly notion?" he said, now rising up to his full height. He wasn't trying to mind his tone now and his voice filled the house. "What do you think? That I simply decided to do this without thinking it through?"

I spread my arms wide to illustrate the ruin of a house.

"You want to know the truth?" Kris asked with a sidelong glance.

"It would be refreshing."

"I've been looking for a way out for months," he said, "ever since last Christmas."

This caught me off guard, but at the same time, I wasn't entirely surprised. I'd known something was amiss. His mood since that night had been as black as I'd ever seen it, but with my head so buried in work I'd never taken the time to do anything about it.

"Why?" I countered lamely.

"They left me no choice!" he shouted, pointing out into the dark. "All of them, everyone who opted not to write a letter. Everyone who let their files be shredded. Everyone who put me, you, us on a shelf because they were too old, too cynical or to 'sophisticated' to care anymore."

For a moment I sympathized with him, but that response just made me angrier. "So that's your solution? Run away? Let the EPA push you around and then go and hide in some broken-down shack? This is *me* you're talking to, Kris, not some two-dollar mall cop on Black Friday. We've been through everything together. War, Depression, empires rising and falling. And the man I know never backed down from anyone. Certainly not some bureaucrat in a bad suit."

"There's more to it than that," he said. "There's a reason people aren't believing anymore, and it's not just the world or the times we live in. We've lost touch, gotten complacent. I'd argue that we don't even know these people anymore. When was the last time you spoke to a child? Can you remember?"

I had to admit that I could not, but in my stubbornness I just turned the question back on him. "Can you?"

"No!" he shouted. "And that's the point! We're out of touch with everything we're supposed to be about. No wonder no one cares! It's obvious we don't!!"

"Then what are you proposing?"

"Well, first thing, we're going to get this place fixed up. And then I'm going to get a job."

"A job," I said. "Like a nine-to-five punch-the-clock…"

"Go-to-work, fight-the-traffic and complain-about-your-boss job," he said with a nod. "It's the only way to get out among the people and learn what makes them tick."

"Boss," I said. "You know I have faith in you, but what kind of job are you going to get?"

"The possibilities are *endless*, Jinn," he said, a twinkle coming to his eye. "After all, who wouldn't hire Santa Claus?"

* * *

As it turned out, it wasn't long before he had his answer. But first we had more pressing matters to attend to. I started the next morning by jumping on the phone with the benefactor whose house we were currently occupying and gently outlining some of the TLC the place was in need of. To his credit, he was apologetic, saying that he hadn't been out to the place in some time, but that he remembered it as being "rather rustic." I rolled my eyes at that one. Calling this place "rustic" was like describing the *Titanic* as having moderate water damage. Nevertheless, I resisted the urge to place a live badger in his stocking and simply asked if he could recommend some contractors who might be able to tidy the place up a bit. Although I didn't love the idea of bringing outsiders into our home, I also wasn't too worried. It's easier for us to walk out in plain daylight than you'd think. Why? It's simple. People see what they want to see. They don't expect to see Santa and his elves strolling down the street in their hometown, so … they don't. To them, the Boss is an ordinary fat man and, if they even notice us elves, we just look like men and women of slightly short stature, nothing more. Sure, the kids do a double take occasionally, but it only takes a quick tug on the arm from Mom or Dad to bring them back in line. So, I wasn't concerned about the contractors, but the sooner they were out of the house, the better. With that in mind, I also called Tenpenny, one of our handiest elves. I had him working in a factory down in Texas assembling rocking horses, but I figured I could spare him for a week or two to oversee the refurbishment. After all, if we were going to turn this place into our makeshift headquarters, we'd have to get cracking.

Tenpenny and his crew arrived a few days later and within two weeks they had the place already on the mend. Carpets were laid down, sheetrock put up, windows refitted, circuits rewired. As I walked in and looked around at the miraculous job he'd done, I realized that we'd given our landlord the best Christmas gift ever, a house that was now easily worth ten times what it had been when we first walked in the door. Some of the other elves wanted to splurge and start calling in favors from all the electronics companies we did business with. There was talk of home theaters, plasma TVs, even a whirlpool bath in the master bedroom. I vetoed all their suggestions one by one. No reason to raise our profile too much. Like I said, I'm not a spoiled elf.

As we were in the process of bringing the house back from the dead, the Boss was on the job hunt. On our first night in New York, he'd wondered who wouldn't hire Santa Claus. Well, the answer was everyone. Occasionally he'd get a call back, but most people simply turned him down on the spot. You could tell it shocked him, maybe even made him feel more useless than he'd already been feeling. Whatever the case was, when he came home after five days of searching with no luck, I saw something in his eyes that I'd never seen before: defeat.

He sat at the kitchen table and sighed. I poured him a cup of hot chocolate, and he downed it in one gulp, waving his hand for a second before the mug had been set down.

"That kind of day, huh, Boss?" I asked, filling the cup for him.

"You said it."

"Well," I said. "You've had the same job for two thousand years. There's not a lot of diversity on your resume. Plus, no real references…"

"I have references," he countered.

I looked at him. "Do you really think that when a prospective employer sees 'Frosty' and 'Rudolph' on a cover letter that they're reaching for the phone?"

He laughed a sullen chuckle and then took a sip from the mug, wincing slightly at the heat.

"Don't belong up there, don't belong down here," he muttered. "Where do I fit in?"

"Look, Boss," I said. "It's summertime, the dog days, you always get down around this time. In a few weeks, school will be back in session and then you…"

That's when it hit me. School! I jumped up, nearly slipping on the linoleum as I did, and raced for the phone book.

"What?" Kris asked, now completely perplexed. "What is it?"

"School!" I said, flipping the pages madly. "School!"

"Yes," the Boss said, nodding slowly as though talking to someone who'd lost every one of their marbles. "School, Jinn. It's where the children go to learn. Now, why don't you sit down and have some of this hot chocolate. I think you need it more than me right now."

I looked up from the phone book. "No, no, you don't understand," I said. "There was a guy, a teacher; gym I think it was. Anyway, he wrote us a letter saying his school was going to close and everyone was going to lose their jobs. I don't remember all the details. But I had a couple of Christmas wishes left over that year that I hadn't granted and so I pulled some strings and made sure the place stayed open. I even got them a grant for some extra money. He wrote me and said that if I ever needed anything, to look him up when I was in town."

"In town?" asked Kris.

41

I slapped the phone book on the table, showing him the entry in the phone book: Haddonville Elementary School. "In town," I said triumphantly. "Just ten short miles from here."

Kris's eyes widened and his face broke out in that all-over grin that only he gets. He picked the book up and looked at the name, reading it and rereading it as if those three words spelled out all the answers.

"This is it!" he said. "This is our ticket! Could it be more perfect? A school, Jinn! Children everywhere: parents, too! I can get a job teaching, maybe woodworking or even science! Who knows more about astronomy than a man who flies around the world by the stars, eh? I can talk with them, learn from them, hear what they believe, what they don't believe. Get a real sense of what's happening. What they're thinking when it comes to us."

I sat back in my chair, placing my feet up on the table.

"It's almost too perfect!" I said.

* * *

Two days later, he came bounding up the stairs sounding like a kid on Christmas.

"Jinn!" he called. "Jinn!"

"I'm in my office," I answered.

More footsteps and then the door banged open and he sailed into the room with a flourish. He was dressed in a grey zip-up jumpsuit with pockets all over. Around his waist was a canvas belt, to which was attached a bevy of keys that jingled as he twirled about, allowing me to get the full effect. On the left breast pocket was stitched an oval patch which had a name written in red script: *Kris*. I shuffled my papers.

"So," I said, a bit wary. "You got a job."

"I did!"

"At the school?"

"You betcha!"

"So, what's with the outfit?" I asked. "Are you teaching auto shop or something?"

"Better," he said. "Ever so much better! They made me—are you ready—the custodian!"

I sat back, stunned. "The custodian. Santa Claus. The custodian."

He bustled about the room, looking like he was about to pop.

"It's ideal," he said, snickering to himself as he did. "I'll be everywhere, cleaning out classrooms, clearing the cafeteria, sweeping the teacher's lounge. I'll talk to everyone, get to know them, I'll be the eyes and ears of that school!"

"Sounds great," I said. "But what do you know about cleaning anything?"

"What's to know?" he said. "You sweep, you mop, you dust. I think I can manage. But…still, maybe you're right. I'd better practice. My first day is tomorrow."

With that, he flew from the room singing "Joy to the World." Before he'd gone too far, his head poked back around the doorframe.

"You were right, you know," he said. "It's too perfect!"

And he was gone again. I sat back and put my hand over my eyes. I really need to choose my words more carefully.

CHAPTER SEVEN

I didn't see much of the Boss during his first few days on the job. I was too busy trying to put out the fires that were springing up all over the place. For starters, the observing teams were in need of a refresher course in the gentle art of subtlety. They'd obviously gotten used to watching from a distance and some of them were having a tough time blending in. There was a report from a team in Tujunga, California, who'd almost gotten pinched after setting up a stakeout in the family's treehouse. Another crew in Moline, Illinois, almost lost a man when he got stuck in a doggie door. And those weren't isolated incidents. Police reports were cropping up all over the country. Little men with binoculars hanging off garden trellises, hiding under parents' beds, sliding down drainpipes. A few more weeks of this and the whole operation would be blown. I'd have to set up a conference call with the team leaders immediately.

The more pressing issue was the goings-on back at the Pole. I'd spoken with Maddox and the news was not good.

"I'm sorry, Jinn," he said. "We're looking into a geothermal conversion, but it's taking a little longer than we'd like to get things up and running."

"Can you give me a target date?"

A pause. "Sometime after the New Year."

"Are you saying the North Pole will be shut down for Christmas?" I asked in a choked voice. "Am I hearing you right?"

44

"I just don't see any other way at this point."

I shook my head. "That's unacceptable, Maddox. Work with our engineers. Find another way. Christmas depends on it."

"I understand," said Maddox.

"I hope you do," I replied and hung up the phone just as the old man came into the room. I checked my watch: 4:30. I had no idea that the day had gone by so fast.

I hadn't seen him for a few days, as I mentioned, and now looking at him, he looked exhausted. His eyes were puffy, his hair unkempt and wild. The jumpsuit he'd so proudly displayed just a few days earlier was splattered with an incredible array of stains, some identifiable, others a total mystery. He sank onto the couch and sighed loudly.

"Long day?" I asked.

There was a pause and then he looked up at me. "Children are such *slobs*," he said in bewilderment. "I cannot believe how much of a mess they make of everything! All day it's clean the gym floor, wipe down the desks, sweep out the lockers. I'll spare you the details of the bathrooms. And their behavior! My goodness, they're like savages. Loud, unruly, and disrespectful! They talk back to their teachers, talk back to their parents; and me? Well, they treat me like some sort of peasant! Do you know how many times I've been hit with a half-full carton of milk by some kid strolling out of the cafeteria?"

"Looking at your uniform, I could hazard a guess."

"And they don't even look back! I had milk dripping from my beard, *chocolate* milk, mind you, and the kid just kept on walking!"

He stood up and began pacing the carpet. "We've been giving presents to these … people all these years? Is this what they've been like all along?"

I shrugged. "They're kids," I said. "You know how they are."

"I thought I did," he said, sounding somewhat dazed.

"Give it some time," I told him. "Either they'll come around or you will."

* * *

The days wore on, and very little changed. Actually, let me rephrase that. Very little changed for the better. If anything, things became progressively worse. On top of all the fires I was putting out around the house and back at the Pole, I had to deal with the old man, whose mood had grown worse than ever.

The biggest problem was the people. Kris just couldn't get a handle on them. He'd try and talk to them, they wouldn't answer. He'd hold the door for them, they wouldn't say thanks. He'd approach a crying child to comfort them only to have a reproachful parent hustle them away, pausing only for a steely glare.

Worse than the everyday people were the kids. As the custodian, Kris was, in their eyes, the low man on the school's totem pole of authority, and they seemed to take great relish in reminding him of that fact. They didn't clean up after themselves, they threw their garbage wherever they saw fit, they wrote words Kris had never seen before on the walls, the desks, their lockers. Stalactites of wet toilet paper hung from the bathroom ceiling, gum clung to the undersides of the tables in the library, papers scattered the hallways like fall leaves. And there to clean up all of it was Kris.

The other morning, Kris told me, the kids were caught having a contest over who could make the cafeteria eggs stick to the wall the longest. After the cafeteria monitor broke up the food-throwing competition, Kris was left to scrape all the scrambled yellow glop off the walls. And, at lunch that afternoon, as a thank you, one of the kids went over to him and barked, "Hey, Tubby, you missed a spot."

"I don't get it," he mused one evening over his usual cocoa. "People used to love me."

"They love Santa Claus," I stressed. "Kris the custodian, however, is just a vaguely creepy old guy."

Kris sat back and stared into the fire. "These people," he asked. "Have they always been like this?"

"More or less," I said. "If you believe what the observers say. But times are tough, too. People are out of work, losing their savings. I went downtown not that long ago, half the shops are closed, boarded up. They don't have a lot to be happy about."

Kris sighed. "I wonder."

"Wonder what, Boss?"

"In a world like this," he said. "Is there even a place for people like us?"

"I think so, Kris," I told him. "Maybe now more than ever."

*   *   *

A few weeks later, I received another call from Tyler Maddox. Actually, it was a conference call. Also on the line were Cog and Flywheel, our two chief engineers, and they were calling to deliver a classic good-news/bad-news scenario.

"How's it going up there?" I asked.

"Well," said Cog, "those EPA boys have the renewable energy system running, wind, solar, the works, and it's burning clean. Remy would be pleased."

"Excellent," I said, pumping my fist in the air. I'd be stoking the fires at the Pole before the weekend. "When can we move back in?"

"It's not that simple," Flywheel interjected. "We've got the system in place, but it ain't turning."

"What do you mean it's not turning?" I asked.

"Just what I said," said Flywheel. "Everything's greenlit and good to go, but it's just not kicking in."

I leaned forward on my desk and rubbed my eyes vigorously. I felt a doozy of a migraine prowling behind my forehead. "It's the magic, isn't it?"

"Bingo."

"The magic?" asked Maddox. "Can you explain?"

"Remember when you visited the Pole in the spring and I told you that a lot of what we did up there ran on magic?"

"I do."

"That wasn't just lip service," I explained. "It's true. Magic is in the air up at the Pole. It's everywhere and, despite whatever conventional means of power we use, magic fuels the whole operation. It's a simple equation. The less magic, the less power."

"So what's the problem with the magic?" Maddox asked.

"Magic isn't self-sustaining," explained Cog. "It's powered by belief. The more people believe, the better it runs. Like Tinkerbell in Peter Pan, the louder the kids clap, the faster she comes back to life. Same principle."

"We've had dips in power before," Flywheel continued. "But they usually balance out. When some people stop believing, a new crop comes in to set the scales right again. But I've never seen a drop-off so severe that it kills the power completely. Something else is going on here. The whole world would have to stop believing for something like this to happen."

Just then, my stomach felt like an elevator with the cable cut. I knew what the problem was.

"So … what?" Maddox asked. "The power's not working because the world's stopped believing in Santa Claus?"

"No, it's worse," I said. "The power's not working because he's stopped believing in himself."

CHAPTER EIGHT

For this next part of the story, you'll have to take my word on things, as I wasn't there to see it for myself. But it's important that I include it because, as you'll see, it all had a pretty large bearing on how everything turned out. Of course, no one saw that at the time. All it looked like was another fight on the playground.

The boss was busy spearing paper on the school's baseball field during recess when a huge quarrel flared up under the basketball hoops. It was pretty intense from what I heard. Two fifth-grade boys going at it full-tilt: Fists flying, curses hurled, the works. At first, Kris saw what was happening and simply shook his head and went back to work. After all, this was now two weeks into his job and his opinion of the kids of Haddonville Elementary had not changed. And this little confrontation was simply further proof that Christmas should indeed be called off, maybe for good.

As the fight grew in intensity, the recess monitor attempted to break it up. Kris happened to glance up as she got between the boys and, the way he tells it, that's when everything began to change. When he saw her, it was as though he was looking through frosted glass that had suddenly been wiped clear. She looked tall and confident, with thick, fiery red hair that seemed to spill down her shoulders. She was maybe fifty or so, but moved with grace and ease of a woman half that age. The monitor got between the boys, who were still throwing punches and waving their arms wildly. A wild swat caught the woman in the chest, not hard, but enough to make her lose her balance and land unceremoniously on the asphalt. That's when the Boss got involved.

He crossed the distance from the field to the playground in about a nanosecond, instantly positioned himself between the two boys. Looking down at them both, he roared at the top of his lungs, "Just *what* is going on here?"

Instantly, the fight halted, mid-swing. When he wants to, the Boss can be downright frightening.

"He stole my DS!" the smaller of the two boys said.

Kris looked down and saw the small video game system clenched tightly in the larger boy's fist. He looked at him, eyebrow raised.

"I was just borrowing it!" the boy protested.

"Did you have any intention of returning it?" Kris said, and the child's downcast eyes gave him his answer. At that point, his attitude softened and he lowered himself to one knee. He looked into the larger boy's eyes.

"You don't have your own?" It was a statement more than a question. There was no accusation in his voice, no blame. Only kindness and understanding.

"I was supposed to get one for my birthday," the child said. "But my dad … he lost his job, and …"

The boy's words trickled off, the tough demeanor dissolved, and the crest of a sob rose in his throat. Kris nodded in sympathy and squeezed his shoulder comfortingly.

"What does your father do for a living, son?"

The boy looked up at Kris. "He's a carpenter."

Kris's eyes widened, and he chuckled softly. "Really? A carpenter. Well, could it be that our meeting is not a coincidence?"

He reached into the pocket of his coveralls and extracted a slightly battered business card, handing it to the boy.

"You have your father call the number on this card," Kris said. "Tell him to ask for Jinn. I think we might have just the job for him."

The boy took the card and nodded, somewhat unsure, but trusting Kris all the same. Kris then turned to the other boy.

"Now, as for you, my good man," he said. "Would you be willing to share your DS with your friend? Just during recess and perhaps on the bus home. Until he's able to get one of his own, that is."

"But ..." protested the boy. "It's mine."

Kris nodded. "I understand," he said. "I know a thing or two about gifts, believe me. But we must never place so much import on the things that we own that we lose sight of the people around us. Otherwise, the things we own will end up owning us instead."

He stood up and turned both boys so they faced each other.

"Now, shake."

Tentatively, the two former enemies reached out their hands and shook. As they did, it seemed that the hostility between them melted away. They walked off smiling together and talking animatedly as though nothing bad had ever passed between them.

The argument diffused, Kris turned to the recess monitor, who'd watched the entire display with a somewhat bemused expression on her face.

"Are you alright?" he asked.

As the woman attempted dust herself off, the heel of her shoe snapped and she lost her balance. Quickly, the old man reached out his hand and gently steadied her. I realize now that that moment, just as their eyes met, was the point at which it all began to go right. Of course, no one saw that at the time, but that's only because things got much, much worse. But still, when I step back and see the big picture for what it is, none of what came after would have been possible had things gone any other way.

The monitor straightened herself out pushed her hair out of her face.

"Yes, yes," she answered, shaking Kris's hand. "Thank you. That was very kind of you."

"Oh that," Kris replied, "That was nothing, really."

"Well, nothing or not, I'm glad you were there, Mr. … ?"

He looked at her blankly a moment, and the way he tells it, it was as if his mind had ceased to turn. The gears and cogs simply came to a halt and all that he was aware of was the space between them. Luckily, he snapped out of it before she noticed.

"Um…" he said, as if he'd just been asked the square root of pi. "I'm…most people call me the custodi…I mean, Kris…most people call me Kris."

"Well, Kris," she said. "Thank you again."

She went to stick out her hand to shake his a second time, and it was only then that the two of them realized that they hadn't let go in the first place. Instantly, they broke from each other's grasp, nervous and fumbling like two teenagers, just as the bell rang.

"I really should be getting…." she began.

"And I should…."

"Right."

The woman turned away, headed back towards the throng of kids streaming towards the school. As she left, Santa called back to her. "Lovely to meet you, Miss … "

"Clara," she said. "Clara Mae Aldridge."

Much later on, Kris confided in me that when he heard her name, he knew that, after so many years alone, he'd finally found his Mrs. Claus.

* * *

It's funny, the moments that divide you. You can be one person for your whole life, and then in a split second, the world around you turns and you are suddenly someone else. Sometimes it's for the better, other times, well, I'm not telling you something you probably don't already know.

Actually, the reason I'm even bringing it up is because, a few days after the fateful "playground exchange," such a moment occurred in the old man's life.

The Boss has always been a bit of an explorer, as you can imagine. You can't spend your entire career circumnavigating the globe without the occasional desire to change things up a bit. So, with that sense of wanderlust firmly in place, he opted to take an entirely different route home from work.

His walk took him down Main Street and he slowed his steps in order to better take it all in. Fall was winding down as November crept closer. The trees had shed themselves of their leaves and the world was covered in an orange and brown blanket hunkering down for the coming slumber of winter. Kris breathed deeply, realizing that in all his years this was the first time he'd ever seen autumn. It was exhilarating.

As he prepared to round a corner, he suddenly ran smack into someone coming out of Alli Oop's, the coffee shop on Main, sending her package of bundt cakes skittering across the pavement as she cried out in surprise.

"Oh my!" said Kris, as he scrambled to the ground in an attempt to salvage the ruined pastries. He brought the crumpled box up and found himself looking into the eyes of the woman he'd met on the playground just a few days earlier. Her fiery gaze softened as she looked at him.

"Kris the custodian," she said, as her mouth played up in a slight smile. "You look lost."

"Clara Mae Aldridge!" he said, unable to conceal the joy in his voice. "How lovely to see you again!"

He then seemed to take notice of the package in his hands and thrust it at her clumsily. "I'm so sorry."

"That's alright," she said, taking the box from him. "It's not my day, I suppose."

"Well, allow me to change that by replacing your purchases."

She shook her head. "Not necessary."

"Of course it is!" he said.

Clara tried to lodge a further protest, but Kris had already clasped her elbow and was leading her back into the shop. He paid for a new batch of cakes and two cups of hot chocolate and carried it all to a table by the window.

"Thank you," Clara said. "You're very generous."

"Think nothing of it," Kris replied.

"Two chivalrous acts in one week," she said. "Not bad."

The Boss shrugged. "I've got a quota to fill," he said, and she laughed.

"I must say, these look good," Kris said, gesturing to the box. "I'm something of an expert on sweets, and these appear to be a cut above."

"Well, you can try one for yourself tomorrow," Clara said. "They're for Samantha's birthday."

"Samantha?"

"Rougeau," said Clara. "Mrs. Rougeau? Third-grade art teacher?"

"Oh, yes," said Kris. "I remember her. About thirty-seven, blond hair. Likes bath salts, if I recall. Crabtree and Evelyn. Two kids, boys, both big *Star Wars* fans. Husband likes golf, has an eighteen handicap."

"Wow," said Clara, "When you get to know someone, you really go all out."

Kris sat back, realizing he'd probably said too much. "Yes, well, it's just that, in my line of work, it helps to know people."

"Your line of work?" Clara asked. "You mean sanitation?"

"No," the Boss replied, smiling slightly. "I mean, before here, in ... my old life."

"What kind of work were you in?"

Kris stroked his beard, trying to gauge what the right answer would be.

"Philanthropy," he said. "Various ... charitable endeavors"

"Uh-huh," Clara said, eyeing him a bit. "And how is it that you came to be here in this little town mopping up after the kids at the elementary school?"

"To tell you the truth," said Kris, as he laughed slightly, "I'm not sure myself. I guess, one day, I just became lost. Or, maybe it wasn't me, maybe it was the meaning of it all that was lost. But whatever the case, I knew that I had to do something in order to find my way again. Lucky for me, my circumstances gave me that opportunity."

"So, this is what, therapy for you?"

Kris took a swallow of his hot chocolate. "Could be," he said. "It could just be. For example, an afternoon such as this. I've never had it before. The time to sit with good company and watch the world go past. Too often it seems as though when the world does pass by, it's at a thousand miles an hour, and by the time I look up, it's already gone."

"Sometimes you have to slow down," Clara agreed, "even just to catch your breath."

"That's what I'm trying to do, Ms. Aldridge," said Kris, "just breathe, even for a moment or two."

They sat a moment in silence, and later Kris told me that the silence was not unpleasant at all. It felt full and rich, an immersion in each other's presence, rather than a retreat from it. Eventually Clara slid the conversation back onto its track.

"Have you missed it?" she asked. "Your old life?"

"Well, I haven't really left it behind entirely," said Kris. "I still stay on top of things, making occasional phone calls, arranging travel plans, that sort of thing."

"You travel in your work?"

"Oh, yes," Kris replied, "all over the world."

Clara sat back in her chair, warming her hands on her cup. "I'm very envious," she said. "It's a dream of mine to head off one day and see the world."

"Have you traveled much?"

She shook her head. "Not really. Wisconsin, where my sister lives. Oh, and once we took a vacation to Long Beach Island. But otherwise, here's where I hang my hat."

"What's kept you?" Kris asked.

"Time, really," said Clara. "It just slips by you, you know? You tell yourself that this is going to be the year you get it done, this will be the year that you keep all those promises you've made. But tomorrow becomes last week and, before you know it, you're flipping the calendar and making all new promises."

Suddenly Kris felt the urge to reach for her hand. Whether the notion was spurred on by the urge to comfort or as a result of attraction, he wasn't sure. Quickly, though, he opted to stifle the feeling as fast as it had come.

"Well," he said, as if conversation might dispel whatever feelings had risen inside him. "You'll have to keep those promises this year! I'll hold you to them."

"I will, I will," Clara nodded, slapping the table lightly to emphasize her sincerity. "I have an old college roommate living in London, and one of these days I'm going to get over there to see her."

"Ah," said Kris, sinking into his chair, "London."

"You've been?"

"Oh, many times."

"What's it like?" Clara asked, "And don't spare any details."

Kris's eyes shone as he talked. His voice lowered to nearly a whisper. "You descend from the clouds through a blanket of London fog. The city is laid out before you like burning embers in a dying fire. Then, as you draw closer, making your way up the Thames, the details slowly come out of the mist. Knightsbridge, the Palace Gardens, Piccadilly. You pass over Buckingham Palace and, if the flag is flying, you give a nod to Her Majesty. Then down to Westminster, where Big Ben rises up to greet you with his lighted face shining in the dark, stalwart and reliable. You make your way up the Thames, over Waterloo Bridge, then Blackfriar and the old London Bridge, until you reach the Tower Bridge. You turn, throwing a salute to the HMS *Belfast*, and make your way back north out to Ealing, Brent, Harrow and Hillingdon, where the houses lay huddled together in the dark along streets tangled like rope. I've seen this world from a thousand different angles, but I'd have to say that sleepy London town holds the warmest place in my heart."

Clara sighed at his description. "It sounds like heaven," she said. "Are you a pilot?"

This last question caught Kris off guard. "Excuse me?" he asked.

"A pilot," she repeated. "From the way you described the city, it sounded like you'd flown over it yourself."

"Oh, a *pilot*," said Kris, as though he hadn't heard the first time. "Yes ... well, I've flown here and there over the years. I still do occasionally. Maybe I'll take you up sometime."

"Oh, no thanks," Clara said with a wave of her hands. "Flying's not for me. I prefer my feet on the ground, where I can always find my footing."

"Interesting you say that," said Kris. "See, my line of work keeps me so busy that when I'm in the air it's the only time I'm ever really at peace."

"Give it time," said Clara. "You'll find your peace on the ground."

He looked across the table at Clara and raised his mug in a slight toast. "I feel as though I'm already on my way," he said.

CHAPTER NINE

A few days after the meeting at the coffee shop, I came into the master bedroom to see Kris decked out in a threadbare suit, with a tatty flower dangling from the lapel. His hair, usually long and bushy, was plastered to his skull by some godforsaken form of gel and he smelled as though he'd showered in aftershave. I stood there in shock a moment.

"I know Halloween's not your holiday," I said. "But if you're aiming to scare the kids on the block, you're off to a good start."

"Don't be cruel, Jinn," he said, linking his cuffs. "It's not in your nature."

"Care to explain the outfit?"

"I," he said, "have a date tonight." He stepped out a bit so that I could take in the full effect. To cap off his eveningwear, he set a moth-eaten fedora atop his head, "What do you think?"

"I think you look like you just escaped from the circus."

"Well, I'm sorry, but I haven't had to dress formal in some time," he said. "These were the best I could find in the luggage."

"That may be, but I can't have you going out like that," I told him, already dialing my phone. "The guys with the butterfly nets will be on your tail in no time."

A half hour later, Kris arrived at Clara's house dressed in a shirt-slacks-blazer combo I was able to throw together after a quick call to one of our observer elves stationed at the mall. Nothing too showy, but enough to keep the old man from leaving the house looking like he was wearing a bum's hand-me-downs.

For their first evening out, Kris and Clara had decided to keep it simple and take in a movie. Out on Route 119, there was the Monsterplex, a multi-screen theater showing every sequel, remake, and TV adaptation Hollywood churned out. But true cinema connoisseurs visited the Ponca in downtown Haddonville. A single-screen movie house, the Ponca showed second-run movies, art-house gems, and classics all for a $5 admission price. This week they were showing *The Italian Job*, the 1969 heist picture starring Michael Caine. Kris was delighted, as Caine is unquestionably his favorite actor. If Kris had any say in who should portray him on the big screen, Michael Caine would get the job every time.

As the movie began, Kris became keenly aware of two things sitting there in the dark. One, the seats were very close together, which put him in closer proximity to Clara than he'd ever been before. Two, there was only one armrest between them. This second fact Kris learned when he went to put his arm there, only to find Clara's already in residence. They both gave a startled jump, muttered apologies, and withdrew their arms immediately. The armrest remained unoccupied for the remainder of the picture.

During the second half of the movie, a group of adolescents, obviously too young to drive themselves out to the Monsterplex, began to make their presence known. They threw popcorn, called friends on their phones and talked to each other in loud, boorish tones more appropriate for a pool party than a night at the cinema. The audience was obviously disturbed, but no one felt brave enough to say anything, and risk fanning the flames of their obnoxiousness. Even Kris tolerated it for a little while, until a hurled bucket of popcorn came dangerously close to Clara's seat. That did it. He rose up purposefully and strode, unbowed, in the teenager's direction. He stood facing them, and spoke in tones of stern warning with an undercurrent of menace.

"If any of you put so much as one more toe out of line," he said, "I will be sure to inform the proper authorities just who's been writing all those creative words on the walls of the third-floor bathroom. What's more, I might just decide to conduct random locker searches to see just who's been trying to smuggle fireworks into the cafeteria."

He stared them down, hands on hips, before driving the point home. "See, I know if you've been bad or good," he said. "That's my job. I'm … *the custodian.*"

The kids' faces fell, their expressions going from disrespect to concern in a microsecond. Kris turned to leave, before rounding on one particularly surly teen whose feet still rested on the seat in front of him.

"An Xbox?" Kris said in disbelief. "After the year you've had? You must be joking!"

The boy's feet hit the floor and he stared at Kris, who returned to his seat to a smattering of grateful applause from the crowd.

* * *

After the movie was over, Kris and Clara decided to take a walk down Main Street. It was a pleasant evening, with the approaching winter's bite still cloaked by the warmth of a slight fall breeze. The wind slipped through the trees like a thief as the clouds turned slowly beneath a lantern moon.

"Pretty tough the way you handled those kids," Clara teased.

"Oh, that?" Kris said offhandedly. "Well, you know, kids are kids. Sometimes you just have to have a firm hand."

"Do you have any?" she asked. "Children, I mean."

"Me?" said Kris. "No, no. Though in my line of work I sometimes feel like I've had a million of them, and watched them all grow up too fast."

"I can relate to that, believe me," Clara said. "That's the life of a teacher. The kids come in, you coach them, support them, give them all you have, then they leave you and it starts all over again. Sometimes I feel like time changes everything around me while I somehow stay the same."

In that moment, Kris felt a kindred connection with Clara. He knew all about the passage of time. He had seen the world when it was young and without shape; he had known the dreams of men when all around them was still ancient stone and empty sky. He had come into their homes as welcome stranger and secret benefactor. But as the years turned on, he would so often arrive to find the beds empty and the hearths extinguished. Time whirled around him like a funnel cloud with him trapped in its eye, unchanged, unaltered, and utterly alone. And yet when he looked into the mirror, Kris came to realize that, in its own way, time had left its mark on him as well.

Just then, Kris felt an overwhelming urge to share with Clara all of these deep and secret things. To open up the hidden places in his heart and lay bare all that had haunted him for so long. Instead, after a moment's pause, he stayed himself and said simply, "I suppose time catches up with all of us."

Suddenly Clara boldly locked arms with Kris, leading him down the street. "Not tonight," she said. "Come on. Sun's up in six hours and the coffee's on me."

And so they went, with the wind eddying at their feet and the night stretched out before them. They talked of things large and small and time did not touch them. For that moment, they stayed as they were … untouched, unspoiled, unbroken. Perfect.

* * *

From that point on, the old man saw a lot more of Clara, though neither would say they were dating in the truest sense of the term. They were just … enjoying each other's company. I think spending time with Clara made the Boss realize just how lonely he'd been. After all, being the sole human in a world of elves and flying reindeer, I imagine it can get to you.

Just so we're clear, Santa's always been a bachelor. Mrs. Claus was created sometime during the 1850s when I found that Santa was tracking better as a married man. He went along with it, but I wonder now if, by keeping up the illusion of a make-believe wife, it just made him all the more aware that he didn't have a real one to come back to every Christmas morning.

Fall began to slowly shed its color and make room for winter. During that time, the Boss spent more and more of his days with Clara and less and less time worrying about our situation. He seemed content to let me handle the reigns on this one. I took it as a sign of his confidence in me, but looking back on it now, I can see that there was more to it than that.

Still, he was in relatively good spirits and it was having an effect. Calls from the Pole were reporting good results. The power was turning, but it was slow and there were still a lot of bugs in the system. As much as I wanted to, we weren't going to be able to get back up there anytime soon.

I resigned myself to not seeing my home for at least a few more weeks and threw myself into our second-biggest bash of the year, the Thanksgiving Day Parade in New York. Yes, second only to Christmas, this was Kris's favorite day of the year. In fact, it might have even rivaled Christmas for first place, because it didn't require any legwork. He simply had to show up and be who he was.

As you might have guessed, Santa can't be everywhere at once, as much as he tries. He makes an effort to appear at every mall, department store and street corner he can, but the world's just too big a place and there are too many people who want to see him. So, on those occasions when he just can't make it, we turn to our "assistant Santas" to fill in. It's not ideal, but it's necessary. But, the one time of the year when you're guaranteed a bona-fide, in-the-flesh, jolly-old-elf Santa sighting, is the Macy's Thanksgiving Day Parade. It's a deal the Boss brokered with Macy's way back when, and he's honored it ever since. I think it's a point of pride for him. Sure, other people have extended offers. I field them every day. But Kris likes sticking with the people who first took him to the dance.

It went as it always did, with the old man bringing up the rear, closing out the parade in grand fashion. I, as usual, laid low. It's not too good an idea for Santa's elves to be running amok down Fifth Avenue with a throng of screaming, eager children. Way too high a risk for exposure. So, I staked out a hotel room high above the street with a good view. Usually, for any public appearance, I have a lengthy checklist that I run through with Kris to make sure he's got everything covered. Entrances and exits, right amount of candy canes, list of probable criers. But today, the rule was simple: just go out and give it your all. Not that I'd need to remind him of that.

It was a perfect day for the parade. The sky was a brilliant blue, streaked with the faintest hint of white clouds like strokes from a painter's brush. The street below was filled with the muted tones of a high school marching band's drum section, the rifle crack of the snares propelled along by the sonorous wallop of the bass. The brass lifted the melody high above the avenue, where, suspended by ropes over the leafless trees, an army of balloon caricatures floated on the morning air, nodding their heads from side to side as if to greet all in attendance.

Along the sidewalk, children waved excitedly from the shoulders of parents, their eyes wide and shining as the colorful procession rolled past. From various holiday-themed floats, smiling singers belted out pop and Broadway tunes with gusto as dancers thumped along in time to the rhythm. Announcers, gloved and earmuffed, called the action enthusiastically from the sidelines, bringing the celebration to life at home for people around the country.

Finally, the big moment was here. I turned away from the TV and went to the window. This one, you wanted to see in person.

The sleigh came down the street and you could feel the energy change in the crowd, passing through them like a current drawn from a socket. The wait was over. We'd been through winter, summer, holidays, barbecues, August sunburns and October hayrides, and it had all led to this. The final door of the year had been opened and the big man was on the other side, waiting to take us to the promised land of Christmas. He was drinking it in. Not because of ego or any reflection of his success or stature, but because he knew that whatever their reasons were, seeing him made people happy, and happiness was what he thrived on.

He stood and waved, "ho-ho-ho-ing" all the way, smiling the million-dollar smile and working the crowd like a champ. Finally, as he reached the end of his route, Kris turned and called out, so loudly that I swear the whole city heard him, "*Merry Christmas to one and all!!!*"

The roar of the crowd was like a tidal wave washing over all of us. For that moment, I forgot about our predicament, about global warming and climate change, about the Pole shuttered and boarded up, and just took in the moment.

Maybe, I thought to myself, maybe it would all work out.

CHAPTER TEN

So, with Thanksgiving behind us, it now meant we were riding the Christmas train full bore and there was no getting off until December the 26th. In fact, it was we elves who first started calling the day after Thanksgiving "Black Friday." The department stores picked up on it and ran with it.

Before we delve into the divine madness that is the Christmas season, all of us take Thanksgiving night to enjoy a huge feast. For many of us, it's the last decent meal we'll eat for a month. The rest of the holidays, we subsist on gingerbread cookies, Pfeffernüsse and Brach's peppermint nougats, all usually eaten on the go, standing on an assembly line or stuffing one package or another into the sleigh. So, come Thanksgiving, we dig into it big time with no regrets. Even though we were eating dinner in a farmhouse in Haddonville, New York instead of back home at the Pole I still tried to savor every bite. Had I known what was about to come, I would have made sure to enjoy it much more than I did.

Usually, the Boss joins us for the feast and shares Thanksgiving with the rest of us. After all, he has to fatten up before Christmas, doesn't he? This night, however, he opted not to sit at our table but had a quiet dinner in the study. He had a guest, you see, and unless you're just joining us, I think you know the person I'm referring to.

The details of the dinner are not important, however. It is what followed that matters most. I wasn't present, mind you, but I have my ways of learning things. How, you ask? Well, the next time someone tells you that they gleaned secret information because "a little bird told them," don't immediately dismiss it as a metaphor.

As you may recall, that was the year that we had that tremendous snowstorm. It started in the early afternoon right around the first quarter of the Army/Navy game and by the time the Jets were kicking their last field goal of the night, the roads everywhere were closed. This was about the time that the old man and Clara were down to their dessert and trading stories. As she reached for her coffee cup, Clara noticed the curtain of white filtering down from the black sky.

"Oh my," she gasped. "Look at it out there."

Kris, for whom this was little more than a dusting, was at first uncertain as to what it was she was referring to. He peered out the window, trying to spot a burglar or errant animal rooting in the garbage. Seeing nothing, he turned back to Clara.

"What is it?" he asked. "Something out there?"

"I should say so!" Clara said, gesturing again to the blanket of snow that carpeted the lawn.

Kris finally caught on. "Oh!" he said. "Of course, yes! Really blowing out there."

"It certainly is," she said. "And I have to get home in it."

"Nonsense," said Kris. "You'll do nothing of the sort. I will take you home myself."

Clara chuckled. "What do you drive?" she asked. "A Sno-Cat?"

A slight smile played around Kris's face and his eyes glinted ever so slightly.

"No," he said, "but I might have something better."

* * *

The two of them trundled out into the storm, bulky and warm in their winter gear, until they reached the barn out back. With a creak and a groan, Kris pried the door open. It was pitch black, but Clara could hear the grunting and pawing of the deer.

"What do you keep in here," she asked. "livestock?"

Kris tapped the flashlight in his hand until the beam snapped to life. When it did, Clara found herself face to face with one of the reindeer, Prancer, from what I hear.

She shrieked, startled, and cartwheeled back. In a flash, Kris was behind her, catching her in his arms.

"It's okay," he said, chortling slightly. "It's okay, he's just saying hello is all."

"You have … " she began, "you have … "

"I have reindeer," he finished for her, "yes, and a sleigh. And, when combined together, they will fashion a perfect means of transport that will take you home."

Still trying to get a handle on the moment, Clara looked around the barn.

"But why?" she asked.

Kris waved a gloved hand. "Call me an old kook, I suppose. Plus, look at me. Don't you think we go together well?"

Clara smiled and shook her head. "You really are a crazy, crazy man."

"That may be," said Kris, then the smile returned. "But I'm your only hope right now."

It took a moment for Kris to get the deer harnessed. He took only two for the ride, Donner and Blitzen, figuring it would be a quick jaunt and back. The others were irritated at being left behind, but he promised them that now, with Christmas looming, they'd be stretching their legs a lot more.

The reindeer properly affixed, Kris then helped Clara into the sleigh and a quick snap of the reins later, they were off.

The world around them was silent, as it always is after a snowfall. It was so quiet that the flakes themselves made a sound as they piled atop one another, like rice being poured from someone's hand. The streetlights glowed yellow, illuminating the snow as it

67

made its descent, and beyond them all was blackness. Clara and Kris were bundled up in the sleigh, with Kris at the reins and the deer trotting ahead, the bells on their harness jingling softly. The sleigh was small, so there was little extra space. As a result, the two of them were sitting close beside one another, nestled beneath the same blanket. If Clara minded, she didn't give any indication. Whether she was grateful for the body heat or the company, Kris didn't know, and he decided not to speculate. Some things are simply better left unsaid and unexplored. Better to just enjoy them at their face value.

A few blocks down, they found their way blocked by a procession of snowplows and sanders clearing the road. Their amber lights and whirring machinery made the deer uneasy. They tilted their heads down, snorting obstinately as their antlers clacked together. The door to one of the sanders opened and a stubby older man poked his head out.

"Hey, pops," he called. "This ain't no place to take a joyride. We've got work to do! Is that thing even street legal?"

"Sorry," Kris called back. "Just trying to get into the holiday spirit, you know?"

"Well, save it for the park, old-timer. We've got roads to plow."

"Will do! Have a good night!"

The driver went back to the steering wheel. "Yeah, you t..." the head came back out. "Hey, do I know you?"

Kris nodded slightly. "I think we might have met before, yes."

The man's demeanor changed and he smiled, revealing a gleaming gold tooth. "Well, you drive carefully, you hear?"

"And you, too, Mr. Tassano."

With that, he turned the sleigh around before Frank Tassano, whose autographed Mickey Mantle rookie card still hung in his den, could stop and ask just how this man knew his name.

They rode along quietly for a moment longer before Clara turned to Kris.

"Who are you?" she asked. "Really."

"What do you mean?"

"I don't know," she said, "but there's something about you. The way people respond to you. How they smile when they see you. It's like you radiate this energy and people just can't wait to get a piece of it for themselves."

"It's the season," he said. "The snow. It does things."

"There's more to the story, I think," said Clara.

But before she could press the issue further, the sleigh came to a grinding halt. The deer were at it again, stubbornly kicking at the snow, steam hissing from their nostrils.

"What is it?" Clara asked.

"Hold on a moment," said Kris and he hoisted himself from the sleigh. He went around to the reindeer and laid a comforting hand alongside Donner's neck.

"What is it?" he asked, keeping his voice low enough so Clara could not hear. "Come on, you can tell me."

Donner snorted and thumped his right hoof at the dirt.

"Been on the ground too long," said Kris, reading his old friend's thoughts, "cooped up. I know. It doesn't seem like it, but I do."

Both Donner and Blitzen looked up and met Kris's eyes.

"You want to fly, don't you?"

The shimmering in their pupils was answer enough. Kris gave them a friendly pat.

"Well," he said, "who better to ask for what you want than Santa Claus, eh?"

He walked back around then pulled himself into the sleigh. Clara looked at him, the confusion creeping back into her face.

"What was that all about?"

"Close your eyes."

"What?"

"Just ... " Kris began. "Just trust me."

Clara did so, albeit somewhat reluctantly. Then Kris leaned forward and whispered the one word it takes to make a reindeer fly. I would tell you what it was, but I'm sure you understand how dangerous it would be if such a word got out.

Of course, using the word was a formality at this point. Once the boys got the OK from the Boss to go airborne, they didn't need a written invitation. Slowly, they began to trot, and then run, then they exploded into a full-bore gallop before, *whoosh*, the ground fell away beneath them.

Higher and higher they climbed until the treetops danced at their feet. Only then did Kris turn to Clara.

"You asked me who I was," he said. His voice dropped to a whisper. "Let me show you."

With that, Clara opened her eyes and saw the lights of the town spread out before her like a jeweled blanket. She started to scream in shock, but all that came out was a slight gasp that rose like scales being played on a single violin string. She reached out and clutched Kris, fearing that she would topple out of the sleigh and fall end over end into the glittering array below her.

"It's all right," said Kris. "Quite all right."

"You mean, you won't … " she said. "they won't … "

"Hasn't happened in all my years on the job," he promised. "And I see no reason why it will happen tonight."

"Then you're really … him?" she asked meekly.

"The one and only."

"I knew it!" said Clara, her fear and shock giving way to excitement. "I think I always knew it!"

"Somehow," said Kris, "I think you did, too."

Clara sat back and watched the town pass below, lights flickering, cars crawling along streets, smoke curling from chimneys. With a quick flick of the reins, the sleigh arced upwards through the clouds and past the storm. Above them were the stars, brighter than she had ever seen them. Below was an endless sea of white cotton.

"So," said Clara, leaning against his shoulder, "what now, around the world? You've done it before in one night, right? Why not tonight?"

Kris laughed his full, rich baritone laugh. "Slow down!" he said. "I've only got two of my boys here tonight. For the full trip, I'd need all eight, sometimes nine."

"So, how far will two take us?"

He looked out at the night sky, trying to orient himself by the stars. It felt good to be in the air again, right in almost every way, righter still with Clara beside him.

"Well," he began, "why don't we find out?"

CHAPTER ELEVEN

They touched down at Clara's house sometime after midnight. Although, truth be told, I don't believe they ever touched down at all.

Now, you would think that having Clara in his life would have solved all the Boss's problems, right? Nope. Actually, it created a whole slew of new ones. It started on my most recent conference call with the Pole. Needless to say, the news wasn't good.

"The power's still not turning up here," said Flywheel. "We've been forced to relocate."

"Relocate?" I asked.

"We're staying at a research station on the ice sheet," Cog explained.

"They're studying polar bears."

"Yeah," Flywheel chimed in. "Did you know their fur isn't actually white? It's transparent. Its hollow core reflects visible light, giving it the appearance ... "

"Let's come to the point, gentlemen," I interrupted. "What's happening at the compound?"

"It's deader than Marley's ghost, man," said Cog. "Can't make it any plainer than that."

"He's right," Flywheel agreed. "There's no way we're having Christmas up here. Maybe ever again."

"I don't get it, though," Cog said. "I thought you said the boss was happier these days."

I felt my teeth grind together like sanding blocks. "Oh he's happy, all right," I said. "And that's precisely the problem."

* * *

Twenty minutes later, I stormed into Haddonville Elementary, intending to give the Boss a piece of my mind. Unfortunately, I didn't get past the front hall before being stopped by a woman seated behind a desk outside the main office. I tried to explain that I was there to see Kris the custodian, but she wasn't hearing it. Like it or not, unless I was a parent here to see a teacher or child, I wasn't getting in.

I was about to lodge a more vocal protest when Kris happened by, pushing his mop and bucket and whistling to himself. I noticed he wasn't whistling a Christmas song a fact that inexplicably served only to irritate me more. His head turned as he strolled past and his eye caught mine.

"Jinn?" he asked. "What are you … "

"We need to talk," I said.

I began to walk over to him and the woman at the desk immediately stood up to block my path. Kris held up a hand.

"It's okay," he told her. "He's with me."

Placated, the woman sat back down, but kept a watchful eye on me as Kris and I walked down the hall.

"What brings you here?" Kris asked. He rolled the bucket down a ways before stopping in front of one of the classrooms.

"Bad things are happening at the Pole," I told him.

"Oh?" He didn't even bother to look up. He just dunked his mop into the bucket and dropped it to the floor with a splat. "You're on top of it, I trust?"

"Yeah, I'm on top of it, but that isn't enough," I said. "The power's not turning up there. The magic, the belief that fuels the whole operation, is ebbing away."

Kris continued to mop back and forth in a lazy, repetitive rhythm. "And what would you have me do about it?"

Now I was getting angry. I snatched the mop from his hands. "Don't you see, Kris? *You're* the problem. First you stopped believing in yourself and now you've let yourself get so carried away with this Clara person that you're starting to forget who you are."

"Please don't bring her into this," Kris said.

"You're the one who brought her into this," I retorted. "Taking her on that sleigh ride, telling her all our secrets. You've been so caught up in this … romance you've allowed yourself to lose sight of everything."

Kris turned away, pacing the floor like a lion before rounding on me with an accusatory finger jutting out. "So, what?" he barked. "I can't be happy for once? After living all these years alone on the ice? After serving every single person on the planet other than myself for my entire existence? I mean, my goodness, I've given joy and happiness to every man, woman and child on Earth! Can't I have some for myself? Don't I deserve that?"

"Of course you do," I said. "But at what cost? Are you willing to give up Christmas just so you can buy a girl flowers?"

"Christmas will come, Jinn."

The hollow way in which he said those words unnerved me. "What does that even mean?"

"Whatever happens, December the 25th will arrive and the children of the world will receive their gifts. Whether those gifts come from me, their parents, or the Tooth Fairy, does it really matter in the end? Is it so important that I tiptoe into their homes and leave the gifts under the tree? No one cares. No one even remembers. The gifts are opened, thank-yous are said and the world moves on. I'm just a servant to them. A hired hand."

"So, that's what you've been in it for?" I asked. "The credit? Yes, you are a servant. We all are. To a pretty high calling, I think. And you used to think so, too."

"You're overthinking this, Jinn," Kris said, waving his hand. "Christmas will come."

"Yes, Christmas will come," I said, "while its patron saint is busy scraping gum off desks in the science lab."

Kris rose up slightly, hackles raised. "That was uncalled for."

I didn't back down. "Your attitude is what's uncalled for. And if your head was a bit clearer, you'd see that."

"I don't need to debate this with you," said Kris. "The reasons I'm doing this are my own, and that should be enough. But let me ask you something. I've been at this for two thousand years. Don't you think I've earned a break?"

Just then, the bell rang. Classroom doors flung open and kids poured out into the hall, elbowing their way past us. If they noticed me, they gave no sign of it. Not that it would have mattered to me if they did at that moment; I was so floored by what I'd just heard that they were almost invisible. I looked at Kris, incredulous. I didn't feel angry, just incredibly dispirited. That he could jeopardize things so badly and then, when called on it, lay such a cop-out answer at my feet, it just took all the fight out of me. I shook my head and nodded to the kids as they nudged by.

"Christmas is less than a month away," I said, thrusting the mop back into his hand. "Take your break on your time, not theirs."

*   *   *

December came and the roller coaster car of our lives reached the top of the tracks. I was busier than ever, making calls, jotting notes, attending meetings, and making appointments. It was an avalanche of work that I wouldn't be digging out from until sometime after the year had turned. Truthfully, I was grateful for the extra workload.

The boss and I hadn't spoken since our little dustup at the school, and having my head buried made for a good distraction.

"How dare they!"

I picked my head up from the Observer's report I was studying as the old man flew into the study, waving a crumpled newspaper with an angry flourish.

"What," I said, "someone forget to print the 'Yes, Virginia' letter again?"

"No, no," he said. "Look ..."

Fwap. The paper unfolded on my desk and I scanned it until my eyes picked up on what had him so upset: a blaring headline: "HADDONVILLE TREE LIGHTING CANCELED."

"Oh," I said, getting it at once. "Yeah, that's a shame."

"A shame?" the Boss fumed. "It's a crime, is what it is. Cancel the tree lighting? It just confirms everything I've suspected about these people. Selfish, totally involved in their own affairs, not caring for tradition, or family or ..."

"Did you actually read it?"

"Excuse me?"

"The article," I said, "did you actually read it?"

"Well, I hadn't gotten that ... "

"Because if you had, you'd see that the reason they're canceling the tree lighting is because they don't have the money."

"What?" said Kris, grabbing for the paper again.

"It says it right here," I said, pointing at the page. "The town's budget is stretched thin this year. Businesses are closing down left and right, Main Street's like a ghost town, there's just not enough money to go around."

The storm in the old man's eyes passed as he gently settled into one of the chairs across from me. He folded his hands into a steeple and rested the bridge of his nose on the tips of his fingers. A grin slowly formed around the ends of his mouth, faint as the smoke from a slow-burning campfire.

"Well, then," he said after a moment's reflection, "that's a horse of an entirely different color, isn't it?"

And that's how, on the second Saturday of December, the townsfolk of Haddonville, New York, found themselves gathered around the largest tree any of them had ever seen, decked out in enough lights to ensure that it could be seen from space, all courtesy of an anonymous benefactor.

As the tree blazed to life and the people cheered, Kris and I looked down from a nearby hilltop high above the festivities and smiled. The strains of "God Rest Ye Merry Gentlemen" played by the local brass band wafted through the night. Kris listened and drew on his pipe, the embers in the bowl glowing red in the dark. He chuckled softly.

"Feels like old times," he said.

"Not so old," I reminded him.

"Maybe," he said, nodding thoughtfully as the smoke rose.

We listened for a time to the merriment down below. The brass band switched to "Ding Dong Merrily On High," followed by "The First Noel."

"Why'd you do it?" I asked.

"What's that?"

"Help these people," I said. "I know they haven't always made you feel welcome."

"I guess I just realized something," Kris said.

"What's that?"

"Maybe these people have a right to be as angry as they appear to be," he said. "After all, how can you keep your faith when piece by piece the world takes away the all the things you believe in?"

I nodded and turned to look at the tree, shining golden against the frozen landscape.

"But," he continued. "That's not the real question, is it? The real question is: How much will you let it take away before you decide to stand up and take something back for yourself?"

He looked at me, peering down from over the tops of his spectacles. "A friend taught me that."

I leaned back against the bench, hands clasped behind my head, tilting my head to look up into the night sky. "Sounds like you've got some smart friends."

A chortle from Kris. "Could be," he said. "Just not too many modest ones."

We both shared a laugh at that.

"Times are tough," Kris went on. "So much so that maybe these people have forgotten what a miracle looks like." He gestured with his pipe to the warm, glowing display down below. "I just thought I'd remind them."

We listened a while longer to the celebration, and as we did, I began to feel better. With this gesture, it seemed Kris had finally turned a corner. Little did I know that, in reality, he was preparing for his final curtain.

CHAPTER TWELVE

It was about a week after the tree lighting that the bottom fell out. Giving that gift to the people of Haddonville had turned the Boss around, or so I thought, but there was still a lot of work to be done. We'd lost time being away from the Pole, and with Christmas Eve nipping at our heels, I needed him to focus now more than ever.

Friday night, I came into his study and found him tinkering away at the naughty and nice lists, trying to figure out a balance between who'd been good that year and who'd come up short. Approximately fifty crumpled pieces of paper lay scattered about the desk. I stood in the doorway a moment before announcing my presence by clearing my throat. He looked up at once.

"Jingles!" he said. "Thank goodness! I can't look at these lists another minute. What's the news?"

"Not good," I said and tossed the newspaper onto his desk.

"What's this?"

"Page six," I said.

The Boss flipped through the paper, scanned the page and then looked up at me, deep concern in his face.

"What does this mean?"

Before I could answer, another one of the elves came in, a worried look on his face.

"It's out there," he said to me. "Local 12's got it."

He snapped the TV on with the remote and we all sat and watched as the anchor recounted the story the old man had just read in the paper.

"The tale of little Sally Buchanan is just the first in a string of reports from all around the county of letters to Santa being returned unopened."

The shot changed to the inside of a mailroom, the camera passing along a long row of overflowing mailbags. As it reached the end of the line, a reporter stepped into frame, his face a serious, somber mask.

"This is the post office in Painted Post, NY," he said, "and for the past week, they have been receiving every letter to Santa sent from the area, all marked 'return to sender.'"

A harried-looking mailman was being interviewed; he had a ruddy face and held his hat in his hands as though he were doing a report on his dog being run over. "Terrible," he said, "just terrible. Hundreds of letters just piled up. It breaks your heart."

Back to the reporter, now walking down the town's Main Street. "And what of the little hearts that will be broken this Christmas?" he asked the camera. "With Santa ignoring their letters, where do they have to turn? It begs the simple question: Why?"

Next, a string of children were interviewed, each trying to answer the reporter's question. They came in rapid succession, one answer following the other:

A boy, 6: "Maybe he's busy."

Another boy, 12: "Maybe he's on vacation."

On and on it went, stopping finally on a little girl, no more than five, her sad eyes looking straight into the lens. "Maybe he's not there."

Pan up to the reporter, now looking more serious than ever. "Maybe he's not there," he intoned. "A question that lingers on all of our minds."

"This is bad," Kris said, sinking back into his chair. "This is really, really bad. How did this happen? Didn't you leave a forwarding address up at the Pole?"

Instantly I knew what had happened, and my stomach dropped like an elevator with the cable suddenly cut. "There were a lot of loose ends to tie up before we left," I said. "Regarding the forwarding address, I delegated that one … to Rags."

Kris's face tightened. "Rags," he said. "That explains everything. Why didn't you just have one of the reindeer do it? Or better yet, Frosty? Sure, he's only made of snow, but that shouldn't be a problem, right? I mean, if you felt Rags could do it, why not Frosty?"

I should take a minute here to explain. Rags is a well-meaning elf, but he tends to get a little … distracted. He comes from one of the wealthier elf families, and he's been somewhat indulged over the years. As a result, he takes very little seriously. Looking back, I should have known trusting even this minute assignment to him was a recipe for trouble.

"He was going to the post office anyway," I said. "He had to pick up a surfboard; said he was going to Cabo for a week. So, I thought …"

"From everything you're telling me," said Kris, "it doesn't sound to me as though you thought at all. Quite the opposite in fact."

"Well, I'm sorry, Boss, but it's kind of tough being the only one running this entire operation," I said. "Sometimes something slips through the cracks."

"You call this 'slipping through the cracks'?" Kris asked. "This is more like swallowed up by the earth! This is nothing short of a total disaster!"

"It could be worse," said Patches, the elf with the remote. "I mean, letters or no letters, the kids'll still get what they want, right?"

"It's not that simple," I said. "This affects the entire way we do business."

"How?"

"It's like this," I began, "the companies we work with, the Apples, Microsofts, Sonys, they separate out their stock, allotting a certain amount to us. Presents from Santa and presents from parents come from two completely different inventories. It makes for easier shipping on Christmas Eve. The companies factor in how many items will most likely come from each list and go from there. If the kids assume that their request from Santa is being ignored …".

"Then they'll just ask their parents for what they want," Patches said.

"Precisely," I nodded, "leaving our contractors with a warehouse full of inventory they can't unload."

"They'll absorb the surplus back into their regular inventory and hope they can make up the difference on President's Day or other sales weekends," said Kris. "But more importantly…"

"They'll cancel our contract," I said, as Kris nodded assent.

"Leaving us dead in the water," he went on. "If we can't rely on those items from the big manufacturers, we're left with either what we can build at the Pole or having to go overseas to lower bidders, which means what we leave under the tree will be … less than the standards we've come to expect."

"A Christmas where Santa is the guy who *can't* get you what you want," I said, exhaling. "We'll be ruined."

Kris sat up, palms flat on the table. He eyeballed me. "Damage control."

"On it," I said. "Already placed the calls."

"Good," Kris said. "We're going to have to nip this in the bud or we're completely sunk."

"Don't worry," I said. "I've got this covered. A few well-placed phone calls and the whole thing will disappear."

* * *

But, as you know, it didn't disappear at all. It grew and grew until it was a monster that no one could control. The media latched onto the "Where's Santa?" theme like barnacles and used it to fuel ratings. T-shirts, bumper stickers, coffee mugs, you name it, showed up on shelves, bearing slogans like "Where's Santa?" and "Do You Still Believe?" and my personal favorite, "We're All on the Naughty List."

Politicians also latched on to the "No Santa" issue, using it as a means to either prey on the public's fears or give them someone to blame for their troubles. One such person was a particularly vocal loudmouth named Evan Kendrick. He was an oil millionaire who had wormed his way into politics and made a name for himself by talking the loudest and bullying the hardest. Word was he was planning a run for the White House in the coming election year, and it seemed as though he was going to try and turn the doubts of the populace to his advantage.

On the night the tree was lit in Rockefeller Center, Kendrick was there, giving an impassioned speech to the masses.

"And in this time of great uncertainty," he said, stretching his black-gloved hands out to the crowd, "all that we have come to believe in has been shattered. But here we stand, shoulder to shoulder, nevertheless, saying, 'We believe.' We believe in a world in which the truth of what we see becomes the truth that we cling to most greatly. We want to believe with our hearts, but only our eyes can be trusted right now. And belief comes from trust, my friends. In troubled times such as these, trust is earned only by offering proof. That is the assurance I can offer you. The assurance that *seeing is believing*. Now, are you ready to believe?"

A cheer rose from the crowd as Kendrick raised his hands high and then lit the tree in a flourish. As the music rang out and the lights twinkled out over 48th Street, Kendrick turned back to face the people.

"And to prove my sincerity," he said, "I'm extending an offer to Santa Claus. If you're really out there, I, along with the good people of this fine city, will be waiting for you on Christmas Eve. I invite you to come here and prove once and for all that you are who you say you are. So, the time is Christmas Eve and the place? Thirty-Fourth Street, a street you once made famous for miracles. Let's see if you can do it again!"

The people cheered and laughed as Kendrick waved and pointed at the screen, calling out the Boss for all the world to see. Disgusted, I flicked the TV off.

"You have to admit," said Kris said to me and Clara, who had joined us to watch the tree lighting, "the man can work a crowd."

"Oh, please," Clara said. "The seventh-grade class president on his worst day could outtalk that clown."

"Doesn't matter," Kris answered. "They're believing him regardless."

"It'll pass," I said. You know it will."

"Maybe," said Kris with a shrug. "And if it doesn't?"

I looked at him curiously. "Not sure what you're getting at here."

"What I'm getting at is that maybe all of this is a sign."

"A sign of what?" asked Clara.

"That my time here is done," said Kris, "that it's time to consider retirement."

"Retirement?" I gasped. "Santa Claus is going to retire?"

"Why not?" Kris retorted. "Most people do so after forty years. I'm going on well over two thousand. God knows I've earned it."

"This isn't a job you just retire from," I said, "take your gold watch and move to Palm Springs. This is a calling. It's a sacred duty …"

"Oh spare me, Jinn," Kris snorted. "I've heard it all before."

"Well, I, for one, am not sure I would like to live in a world without a Santa Claus," said Clara.

"I'm retiring, my dear," said Kris. "I'm not dying."

"And what about the children of the world?" she asked. "Where do they fit into your little plan?"

"The children of the world don't need me," Kris replied. "They have Mom and Dad, Toys R Us, Amazon and eBay. They'll get along just fine."

He walked over to his desk and started flipping through his Rolodex. After scanning the cards, he found what he was looking for. Scooping the phone up, he dialed, then after a few cursory rings, he spoke up.

"Paulie?" he said, and I knew what was going on. Paulie was in charge of gift production for North America. In the state of mind Kris was in, a call to Paulie was not going to have positive results.

"Don't do this, Kris," I said. "Don't let people like Kendrick get you riled up and do something you'll regret."

"Paulie," said Kris, ignoring me. "I want you to shut down production immediately. No, that's right, you heard me. Shut it down. What's that? Yes, indefinitely. No … just … just do what I say. Thank you."

The phone fell back into the cradle and Kris looked at both Clara and I.

"You're making a terrible mistake," she said. "People still *want* to believe."

Kris stood up and walked to the door. "Maybe they do," he said, "but what if I don't?"

With that, he turned on his heel and slammed the door behind him. A heavy silence fell in his absence. I turned to Clara. "He's usually a lot more jolly this time of year."

* * *

There was no changing Kris's mind. It was over. I pleaded with him for days on end, but his mind was made up. I tried to get him to see it as an opportunity, a chance to capitalize on people's lack of belief by giving them something to believe in. He didn't want to hear it, though. In his mind, the people of the world had let him down, and Kendrick and his followers were the proof. They'd sent him a message, and to him it was loud and clear.

So, I was left with the unenviable task of pulling the plug. One by one, I ordered gift production shut down around the world. The elves were shocked at the news, and I told them they were all welcome to come to the house, where they could stay until we figured things out. Returning to the Pole, however, was out of the question. The power had been out for weeks and now, with Kris refusing to take up the role of Santa Claus, it was likely that it would never come on again. Flywheel and Cog went up there for a cursory check and came back with a grim report. Water had seeped through the walls, blistering the paper and soaking through the carpets. The hallways, once warm and inviting, were dank, unwelcoming passages that snaked on into impenetrable blackness. Fireplaces were barren, extinguished. Statues of Christmas characters stood hollow-eyed and alone, looking out over the ruin of their empty, forgotten estate.

"It's weird," said Flywheel. "We've only been gone for a week or so, but by the look of the place, you'd think it's been years."

"I don't know," I said with a shrug, "maybe as our dream is dying, the Pole is dying with it."

A few days after my phone call with Flywheel, the boss and I headed out into the early morning air, crunching our way through a mantle of snow lit up by the orange sun. Approaching the barn, Kris threw his shoulder against the door, pushing it open as the hinges protested.

"Are you sure about this?" I asked.

"Yes, I am," said Kris. "It's what's best for them."

We herded the deer out into the yard until they were standing in a crowded semi-circle, huffing angrily at being awoken so early. After a moment's pause, Kris reached into his pocket and withdrew a pistol. Don't worry, it was just a starter pistol. No bullets. He didn't need them. Not for what he had planned.

With a heavy sigh, Kris raised the pistol. He held it over his head and fired one shot up into the air. Startled, the deer scattered in a clatter of hooves and antlers. They ran pell-mell in a circle until Kris fired a second shot. That was all it took. The deer made a break for the fieldstone fence at the far end of the property, clearing it in a single leap.

The leaves rustled and the underbrush crackled as one by one they disappeared from view.

As he watched them vanish into the thicket of trees, Kris stared ahead, his eyes fixed on one point in space, his jaw set but trembling slightly. I stayed with him there in that snow-covered grass for a while longer, looking out into the woods beyond, but I did not speak. What was there left to say?

* * *

After letting the reindeer go, Kris walked into the kitchen, stamping the snow from his boots. He looked up at the house, now completely empty, shucked his gloves from his hands and sighed. Behind him, he heard the sound of a throat being cleared. He looked over his shoulder to see Clara standing there in the doorway.

"Sorry," said Kris. "I didn't hear you come in. Did you need something? I could have Jinn …"

"I came to say goodbye," she said, cutting him off.

Kris looked at her, eyes wide. "What?" he asked. "Why?"

"You're not the man I fell in love with."

"Because I'm not Santa Claus anymore? Sorry to disappoint you, Clara."

"Oh, you disappointed me," Clara said. "Not because you're not Santa Claus, because you chose to give up who you are without a fight."

"I didn't give up!" Kris protested. He pointed outside. "It was them, everyone out there who …"

"Keep pointing your finger, Kris," said Clara. She spread her arms wide. "But if you look around you'll see you left yourself with no one else to blame."

She turned to leave. Kris pushed his chair out and stood up.

"Clara, I …"

"Merry Christmas," she said, as a choked sob bit off her words.

As the door closed behind her, the old man was left alone, consumed by the reality of what he had done. His legs felt watery and he clutched the table and eased himself back into the chair. The silence of the house filled his ears and a sudden and unimaginable grief washed over him. For the first time since he had become the man the world knew as Santa Claus, sitting there in that kitchen with only the ghosts of his past for company, Kris Kringle slowly put his head in his hands and wept.

CHAPTER THIRTEEN

It should have ended there. I mean, from where I was sitting there was no way to make things right at that point. Most of the elves had moved on, some back up North, where they had families living outside the Pole, others to new homes around the country. The deer were long gone, living wild in the woods somewhere. Clara was gone and the Boss was more depressed than ever. He still had me, but what good was I? My job had always been to take care of Santa Claus, and that man didn't exist anymore. Yes, there was no question about it. It was over. But, as you know, Christmas is that funny time of year where things that would never happen at any other time just seem to happen all on their own. It started at school.

Now that he was no longer Santa Claus, Kris was destined to be the Haddonville Elementary School custodian for the rest of his days. Three months ago, that prospect would have filled him with dread. Now he accepted it without question. In fact, I think he liked going to that school every day and cleaning up after the kids. It made him feel useful.

In the days and weeks leading up to the holidays, the kids had been as wild and unruly as ever. But then, just as the world began to wonder what happened to Santa Claus, something unusual happened. Kris found that he was cleaning up fewer messes. The graffiti disappeared entirely. The food fights ceased at once. The halls sparkled, the bathrooms shone, the desks gleamed. Kris didn't understand it at all, until Clara, breaking the spell of silence that had gone on between them since her departure, laid it out for him.

"Don't you get it, you silly old fool?" she chided. "They're being *good*."

And so they were. Whether they'd gotten together and decided as a committee or were each acting on their own, he did not know. But the fact remained that the children of Haddonville, and, as we learned, around the world, had cleaned up their act. In one school, a particularly enterprising young child had created buttons and handed them out to everyone in her neighborhood. They were simple, but effective, an image of Kris standing against a solid white background. Beneath the picture, in large green letters was one word: *Believe*. Like I said, simple, but effective.

Late one afternoon, Kris was busy shoveling snow from the front walk of the school when he felt a hand slide into his coat pocket. He turned and saw a little boy walking away towards his mother's car, not looking back at all. Kris reached into his pocket and extracted a crumpled sheet of loose-leaf paper. On it, scribbled in crayon, was a Christmas list. As he looked at the paper, a thought passed through his mind like a cold wind through an empty house.

Had they always known?

But what was happening at the country's schools was just the beginning. Everywhere Kris went, he saw something that made him pause a moment and think. People caroling on doorsteps, gathering food for the homeless, clothes for the needy. Random acts of kindness that sprung up from the frozen ground like stubborn flowers.

"What does it mean ... 'You've been Claused'?"

I looked up from stoking the fire in the den. "Huh?" I asked.

"'You've been Claused,'" he repeated. He was standing over me, stroking his beard, but his gaze went past the room, out to somewhere in the middle distance. "I overheard someone saying it down on Main today."

"Oh," I said, standing up and tossing the poker back in its holder. "It's something they've been doing around town. You know, you leave something for someone on their porch or in their car, something they need, food or whatever, but you don't tell them you did it, you just leave a note saying, 'You've been Claused.'"

"Really," he mused, his hand running the length of his beard again.

"Yeah, you know, like you … like you used to do."

He didn't answer that one but simply nodded, walking out of the room with heavy, thoughtful footfalls.

A few days later, he and I were walking home from the market on Demarest after the Boss discovered he was out of chestnuts. We walked home, bundled up against the cold, Kris clutching the paper bag under his arm as the wind whipped around us. A few wayward flakes swirled through the air, bounced along by the pre-Christmas gale.

As we moved along the streets, the sights and sounds of the town surrounded us. We noticed a sign soaped into an empty shop window, an arrow pointing up with the words, "Kris Kringle, Plenty of Landing Space Up Top!" Sidewalk Santas clanged bells as passersby plunked change into their red buckets, hurrying down the sidewalks with bags of presents straining in their fists. At the corner, a street musician dressed in a tatty elf suit strummed an electric guitar, singing a cover of Darlene Love's "Baby, Please Come Home," replacing "Baby" with "Santa."

The scene downtown did not pass unnoticed by Kris. As we headed up the hill and out of town towards the farmhouse he looked over at me.

"Remarkable," he said.

I shrugged in response. "It's like I've always said, Boss," I told him, "if you didn't exist, people would have to invent you."

"What's that supposed to mean?"

"Look around you," I said. "It's a hard world. I mean, we live in a magic castle with elves, talking snowmen and bowls of candy that replenish themselves. These people, some of them have lives so hard it's a struggle just to get up every morning. But this is the time of year that most of them can put that aside and try and seek out some joy in

91

the world. And if you're not there to do it, they'll turn to someone else who will. And that's where the Evan Kendricks of the world come in."

The mention of Kendrick and his dare darkened his mood. Kris clutched the bag tighter, increasing his stride. "I won't be bullied into being Santa Claus, Jinn."

"Why not?" I said with a shrug. "You let yourself be bullied out of it."

Having no answer for this, Kris simply stared ahead and walked onward towards home, leaving the lights and sounds of Haddonville behind him.

CHAPTER FOURTEEN

Right before the last day, on December 23, a bona fide miracle happened. You would think that in my line of work I'd be able to spot a miracle from a mile out, but sometimes these things just catch you off guard.

Kris and I were walking down the back stairs of the farmhouse heading to the garage to load up the SUV I had rented for us. We were going to spend one last night at the house, then head out on Christmas Eve. The Boss had already booked tickets to Bermuda.

There we were in the driveway when the old man heard footsteps crunching in the snow behind him. He whirled around and saw Prancer standing there, pawing at the ground gently.

"Well, hello there," said Kris, unable to keep the slight smile from spreading over his face. "What are you doing here? I thought we let you go."

He looked at me for an explanation, but I could only throw up my hands. "You ever try to get rid of a faithful dog?"

Kris's tone became a bit more insistent. "Come on now," he said. "Go!"

He gave Prancer a gentle shove, but the reindeer wasn't moving. He stood his ground, all four hooves locked into the snow, and snorted defiantly.

"He doesn't want to let go," I said. "I can understand how he feels."

Kris grappled with the reindeer a bit more but he could see he was on the losing end.

"Okay, okay," he said. Then he reached into his many pockets and fumbled about for something to give him, finally extracting a carrot. He extended the offering to Prancer, who gingerly took it. As the reindeer ate, Kris patted his snout.

"You're a loyal old friend," he said. "but nevertheless … "

Before his thought could be finished, the screech of car tires could be heard from the road. All of our heads, including Prancer's, snapped up.

"What was that?" Kris said.

"Someone at the end of the driveway," I said.

"Did they see us?"

"Not sure," I said. "It looked like someone was leaning out the passenger window, but I couldn't tell for certain."

"Probably nothing," said Kris.

We didn't ponder the mystery of the car any longer, but it was okay, because someone else did the legwork for us, and by the time the six o'clock news aired, we had all the answers we needed.

"Santa Claus has been found!" the anchor said, smiling wider than ever. "This video, taken with an iPhone in upstate New York, shows what looks to be the man in red himself, feeding one of his reindeer."

"Uh-oh," I said.

"What does it matter?" said Kris. "It's a gag piece, something hokey for the holiday ratings."

The anchor went on. "This sighting fuels hope that maybe children will see Santa after all this Christmas Eve."

"You were saying?" I said.

"Who cares?" grumbled Kris. "Fluff journalism, that's all. Who would take that nonsense seriously?"

But when morning came, Kris had his answer. As the sun rose, he went out, groggy and bleary-eyed to grab the paper, only to be greeted at the gate by a throng of people, all cheering, holding signs and singing "Santa Claus is Coming to Town" at the top of their lungs.

Kris backpedaled as fast as he could and raced into the house as the crowd snapped pictures with their cameras and cell phones. Once inside, he looked at me as I walked into the front hall.

"Something up?" I asked.

"It's Grand Central Station out there," gasped Kris. "What are we going to do?"

"You could always go and say hello," I said. "They did come to see you, after all."

"They came to see a curiosity," said Kris. "We'll wait them out. They have homes, and they'll go to them soon enough."

"Leave Santa's house on Christmas Eve?" I said. "I wouldn't be so sure."

"You think they'll stay out there all day?"

"I would."

Turns out I was right. The crowd not only stayed put, it grew. All day, the carols rang out, the cheers and chants filled the air. Local news vans rolled up and set up shop on the lawn, the reporters delivering the play by play as the shadows lengthened on the lawn. Finally, as the darkness fell and Christmas Eve was upon us, the tone of the crowd changed from raucous to somber. Looking out the front window of the farmhouse, Kris saw hundreds of candles being lit at once as the gentle lilt of their singing rolled over the snow-covered lawn to meet his ears.

"*O, Holy Night*

The stars are brightly shining ... "

Kris stood and listened to the singing, dumbstruck, unsure of what to do. Suddenly, he became aware of someone behind him. He turned to see Clara timidly walking into the room.

"It's Christmas Eve," she said with a shrug. "What better time to make up?"

Kris looked over at me as I stood in the doorway, then smiled. What can I say? I know what the Boss needs. It's why I've stayed employed for so long.

I ducked out as Clara sidled up next to him and joined him in looking out at the people standing outside.

"When I was a little girl," she said, "my father played Santa every year at our family holiday party. I never questioned that he wasn't the real thing. It never occurred to me that, when Santa was there, my father wasn't. I just believed. Years later, after my father had died, I was looking for his pocket watch in his closet and I found the Santa suit still hanging there. Just hanging there right next to his three-piece suits, his crazy Hawaiian shirts and the cardigans he wore over his pajamas when he went out to the market late at night. Now, you would think that a moment like that would take everything I believed about my childhood and force me to question it, wouldn't you? But you know what? It made me believe even stronger in the magic of Christmas. It made me realize that, young or old, there's still room in your life for extraordinary things. And if they don't happen, then you go out and make them happen. Magic doesn't have to be supernatural. It simply has to come from inside you, from the well where all our beliefs lie, and if you try hard enough, that well doesn't ever need to run dry."

"Fall on your knees!

O hear the angels' voices.

O night, divine ... "

Clara looked over at Kris and saw a single tear roll down his face. It was not from sadness, she realized, but an overflow from the flood of emotions that now coursed through him. She reached over, lacing her fingers with his.

"These are terrible times we live in," she said. "The things we believe in are called into question every day. Our leaders, our values, our own way of living. But here, at this time of the year, we dip into that well, into whatever may still be left there, in the hopes that we might draw from it something that will carry us through. That's why these people are here."

Kris looked out into the candlelit display on the lawn.

"They're not here for me," he said. "They're here because of something they saw on the news."

Clara shook her head. "They're here because there's a chance that Santa Claus, the *real* Santa Claus lives here, and they want to see him. Santa Claus is more than just one man, even a man like you. He's proof that the magic we hear about as children really exists, and that the bright lights of our youth don't go out when we grow up. And they want that to be true so much, especially now. Because if you're real ... then *anything* is possible."

Kris looked uncertain. "I don't know ... "

"What's there to know or not know at a time like this?" asked Clara. "This is one of those moments where you don't think, you just believe. And these people? They just want to believe in something, even if it's just for tonight."

She nudged him playfully but firmly.

"So go," she said. "Go out there and make believers out of them."

Gently, Clara took his face in her hands and met his gaze.

"Go and make one of yourself."

Kris looked at Clara and saw in her eyes a reflection of himself, a glimmer of the man he used to be, and the man he had become. The years unwound in that moment like twine rolled across a hardwood floor. The early days, traveling through the woods on the back of a goat, the carolers calling out "Goday, Sire Christmas!" The bells of Yorkshire, pealing as he descended over rooftops to see the Yule candles blazing in the windows. All through the ages it was the same: the people laughing, beating on homemade instruments, the holly and the ivy intertwined, strung about in merry ropes across warm rooms where families gathered. The songs that rang out from door to door as the revelers went wassailing out into the night. And the children, always the children, with their wide, all-believing eyes and pure, unfettered hearts, shaking parcels beneath the tree, popping Christmas crackers to race about the house in paper crowns as the hearth crackled merrily. And here he was, at the other end of a long season of ages, and still it was the same, the carolers, the revelers, the believers, lined up end to end in hopes of glimpsing that ever-elusive something that seemed to remain hidden the rest of the year. "Christmas will come," he had said. And so it had. What a fool he had been to believe he could ever make it otherwise.

Inside his chest, his heart swelled like a rose blooming after a spring rain. He looked at Clara, his eyes alive with light.

"I believe," he said, laughter bubbling up from deep inside him. "I believe in Santa Claus!"

She laughed along with him and embraced him warmly. "So do I," she said. "I always have."

Twenty minutes later, Kris strode into the kitchen, resplendent in red and white.

"What are you doing sitting around, Jinn?" he said. "It's Christmas Eve."

"It's about time," I said. "So, what's your plan?"

"Well," he said. "I've got no sleigh, no reindeer, and no presents to deliver, so my plan is basically ... well, I was hoping you might be able to help me with that."

I stood up and walked to the back door. "I think I know just what to do."

The door opened and Kris's eyes went wide as he saw his old sleigh, polished up and ready, piled high with gifts. In front were all eight reindeer, standing at the ready, awaiting takeoff. Kris was stunned.

"How did you ... ?"

"For the sleigh, you can thank the kid from the playground," I said. "His dad isn't just a carpenter; he's an artist. And the deer? Once Prancer came back, it didn't take too long for the rest of them to find their way home."

"What about all these gifts?"

I shrugged. "I called in a few favors with some of our old clients," I said. "A few centuries of goodwill goes a long way, you know?"

Kris laughed as he shook his head. "I suppose it does."

He climbed into the sleigh, looking back at me for one final salute.

"You were right, you know," he said. "They never stopped believing."

"Neither did I," I replied.

Seated there at the reigns, Kris looked at home, in place. I saw the glint that had returned to his eyes, the glow that hung around him like an aura.

"Where you headed?" I asked.

"Around the world, of course," he said. "But first, New York. There's someone who wants very much to see me, I think."

We laughed. It was good to have my friend back.

"Say it," I said. "You know you want to."

"Oh, very well," he relented, then took a deep breath and called out. *"HO! HO! HO! MERRY CHRISTMAS!!"*

The crowd outside cheered in response, as the sleigh began to slide along the lawn, gathering energy. Hooves churned up the snow underneath as the runners slid along the ice at the base, making an insistent noise like a thousand voices *shushing* at once.

"Go baby go!" I cried out, raising my hands triumphantly above my head.

Faster and faster they went until, like a rocket, the sleigh took off, trailing stardust behind it. Over the heads of the crowd Kris and company flew as they hollered ecstatically, faces turned upwards, arms outstretched.

I reached into my pocket, grabbed my phone and dialed Cog and Flywheel.

"Get back up to the house and start getting the place prepped," I shouted. Overhead, Kris sailed off into the icy darkness, iridescent rainbow-colored sparks shimmering in his wake. "We're not gong to make it for Christmas, but it's going to be one heck of a New Year's."

CHAPTER FIFTEEN

Once in the air, Kris steered the sleigh towards New York. The lights of the City soon flickered below him as he guided the reindeer down below the clouds. Right on 34th Street, our old pal Kendrick was waiting, riling the crowd up at the prospect of Santa's no-showing the event.

"On Christmas Eve, we stand now as a people united not by our childish clinging to outmoded beliefs, but in our conviction that we, as a people, stand for what is real and true and honest. Remember, my friends, *seeing is believing*!!"

At that precise moment, in a move that couldn't have been better timed, Kris swooped down directly over the heads of the crowd, hurling candy canes down from the sleigh and calling out "Merry Christmas" in his most booming tone of voice. The people on the street roared in approval, waving frantically as Kris flew by.

Smooth as silk, Kris turned the sleigh around and did the last thing anyone would have expected. He set it down right smack in the middle of the street.

The cheers of the crowd fell silent as everyone tried to process what they were seeing. Was it a hoax? An elaborate special effect? A publicity stunt from Macy's? Or maybe, just maybe, the real deal?

Kris stepped out of the sleigh and strode up to the podium. Kendrick was pale and speechless. This was most decidedly not in the script. As Kris approached him, he attempted to lodge a protest, but all that came out was a cadence of stammered syllables that sounded like "Buh, Buh, Buh … "

"May I?" Kris asked, gesturing to the microphone, and Kendrick merely moved his head up and down, signaling assent.

"Thank you," he said, and then turned to face the crowd.

"Good evening," he began. "And, of course Merry Christmas."

The crowd murmured "Merry Christmas" in reply, still somewhat shocked, but warming to the moment.

"I'm sure you're wondering what I'm doing here," said Kris. "Frankly, so am I. But something told me that I had to be here, I had to say out loud what I've been feeling for so long, if only so that it made sense to myself.

"I know I've been away for a time," he continued. "But even though I've been gone, I … I haven't really left. I've been right here among you; and I'm grateful that I've had the chance to be . Because, even though I've been coming into your homes all these years, I don't think I ever really knew you.

"But in recent months, the more I got to know you, and I have to be honest here, the less I liked you. I thought you were petty, spiteful, and ungrateful people bouncing madly about in tiny prisons of your own construction, trapped by your greed, your avarice, your incessant wanting. It seemed you all felt the world owed you something, a debt to be called in simply as a result of your mere existence. And at first I sneered at you, sitting there in your little cells. Until, that is, I realized that … I was no better. Because, you see, I had constructed a prison of my own, a place where I could lay the blame for my shortcomings squarely at the feet of others. And I'll tell you, it can be wonderful, for a time, telling yourself that life would be so perfect were it not for the blunderings of everyone else around you. The problem is, with only yourself for company, eventually you'll hear only what you want to, and not what you sometimes need to."

He paused, looking down at everyone, taking in their faces and seeing the mixture of awe and disbelief that crossed them.

"Have you ever stepped outside late on Christmas Eve?" he asked. "Late at night after all the eggnog has been drunk, all the relatives have gone home until tomorrow? Maybe you realized you have to get that quart of milk for breakfast or run one last errand to ensure everything is prepared for the morning, or maybe you have to take the dog for a quick turn around the block. Whatever the case, when you do step outside, you feel the quiet. That total perfect stillness. And in that stillness, if you take a moment to listen, you can hear it."

Everyone leaned in slightly, as though listening for whatever it was the old man wanted them to hear. He gazed out at them over his glasses, smiling.

"The heartbeat of the world," Kris said. "In that moment, whether we believe or not, whether we celebrate Christmas or not, the world is quiet, the talking and noise has ceased, the fury and riot of everyday life has retreated for a moment into the dark and, for that brief instance, we are truly at peace. If only we could live in that quiet a little longer, maybe this world wouldn't be so bad.

"We all lose faith once in a while," he went on, "even me. But if we search out that shared heartbeat, for all the other hands out there groping in the dark, then suddenly that darkness doesn't seem so all-consuming. And that's the real magic of Christmas. It shines a light into the unlit corners of our lives and reminds us that, whether we realize it or not, we're all in this together.

"It took me some time to realize these things, mind you," Kris went on, "but I hope that my sharing them with you here tonight has brought you some comfort. Consider it my first Christmas gift of the year. I hope you can forgive its late arrival.

"After all," he said with a slight chuckle, "I may be immortal … but I'm only human."

Kris stepped back from the podium and glanced at his watch.

"Goodness!" he said. "I have to be going. Christmas won't wait, even for me."

He raced back to the sled, grabbed the reins, and rose up slowly before hovering a moment. Then, leaning over with a wave, Kris called out to the crowd.

"Happy … "

" … *CHRISTMAS TO ALL AND TO ALL A GOOD NIGHT!!!*" they yelled back to him before erupting in a chorus of cheers and applause. Over their heads, the sleigh took off at full speed, curving through the canyons of the city before banking out over the river and disappearing from view.

* * *

From Manhattan, I guided Kris to a small airport outside of town where we could make final preparations for the flight around the world. We were going to have to double- and triple-time it, since the sun would already be about to come up in certain areas.

We'd set up shop in a hangar at the far end of the airfield. Inside, it was a hubbub of activity, with elves running to and fro, reading weather reports, checking flight paths of other aircraft, scanning the news. The airport had been generous enough to spare some of the tower crew for the night and they were busy studying the radar, their faces bathed in green light.

As I walked around making final preparations, I saw that some other people had joined the party. The elves that had been staying out at the house, had arrived and brought with them enough provisions to stage a pretty decent Christmas party. Cookies, homemade fudge, pastries and pies were stacked high, looking delicious and inviting. Cakes dripping with frosting and shimmering bowls of candy lined the tables from end to end. Jugs of eggnog, pitchers of warm cider and bubbling pots of hot chocolate were filled and refilled as revelers drank to their hearts' content. A few of the backup deer had shown up as well and were click-clacking about, nosing carrots out of generous hands. Someone had set up a tree in the corner and lights were strung about the room, bright white and glowing warmly. The mingled smell of pine and gingerbread filled the air as Christmas music blared over the loudspeaker, putting everyone in the right frame of mind.

"Jinn?"

I turned around and saw Harry Beecher, the carpenter who had repaired the sleigh. I grinned and stuck out my hand, which he gladly took.

"Harry!" I said. "Glad you got my invite. After everything you did for the sleigh, it's only right that you're here to see her off."

"It was my pleasure, really," he said. "Have you met my family?"

I shook hands with his wife, and then looked down at his son, Tim, the same one Kris had seen fighting on the playground so many months ago. I smiled at him.

"You know, kid," I said. "If you hadn't told the Boss your dad was a carpenter, the sleigh might never had flown again. You're gonna go down in history as the boy who saved Christmas!"

The boy beamed, his face going red as his parents hugged him and laughed.

"Well, listen, Jinn," said Harry. "You've got my number. If you ever need anything else, I'm happy to help. I don't just do carpentry. I can do electrical, plumbing, ventilation, whatever you need."

"Really?" I said, eyebrows arching. I thought of the Pole and its current state of disrepair. "How do you like the cold?"

Before Harry could answer, another hand jutted out from the crowd and grasped mine.

"Mr. Jinn, it's an honor, sir," said the hand's owner, a plump, round-faced man wearing a suit with a brilliant red tie.

"Thank you," I said, as my right arm went up and down like a jump rope. "Thank you very much, Mr. … ?"

"Braithwaite, James William Braithwaite," he said. "The third. I'm the mayor of Haddonville."

My smile brightened. "Mr. Mayor," I said. "Well, then, the honor is all mine!"

"I hope you don't mind my crashing your party," Braithwaite said. "Harry's an old friend and when he mentioned he was coming…well, I just wanted to thank you for all you've done for our little town. People are just buzzing about our … ahem … famous resident. I hear that the Lamplighter Inn's booked through New Year's! Patty Deane down at the Junebug called me this morning to say she was taking reservations. *Reservations!* Can you believe it?"

"That's wonderful news," I replied. "We're just happy to see the town get its due."

"Well, sir," said Braithwaite. "That's what I wanted to talk to you about. I was hoping you and I might have a little … ah … discussion about some … entrepreneurial possibilities that might exist between our two camps."

I cocked my head. "Meaning?"

Mayor Braithwaite spread his hands out wide, emulating a billboard. "Haddonville, New York, Santa's home away from home," he said, capping it off with a million-dollar grin. "You gotta admit, it's got a nice ring to it."

I laughed out loud with a shake of my head. I liked the way this guy thought. Reaching into my pocket, I handed him my business card. "Give me a call after the holidays," I said. "We'll talk. Don't worry, Mr. Mayor, I have a feeling business in Haddonville is about to pick up."

We shook hands and parted company. Just then, Kris touched the sleigh down, sending sparks from the runners along the hangar's smooth floor.

"Where've you been?" I said, racing over. "Thought you'd wait till Boxing Day to deliver the gifts?"

"Keep your shirt on, Jinn," said Kris, sounding more and more like his old self. He climbed out of the sleigh and took stock of the goings-on around him. "What's the situation?"

"It's 11 o'clock in London," I said. "You can still make it, but then you're going to have to do a fast turnaround to get back here before dawn."

"Got it," he said. "What about flight patterns?"

"With everything going on I didn't have time to get NORAD anything accurate," I said, "but I gave them my best guess. Nevertheless, they recommended that you fly with a little help this year."

I gestured to the two F-22 Raptors sitting on the tarmac. A pair of ramrod-straight pilots strode from the jets and snapped two firm salutes at Kris.

"This is Captain Kendall and Captain Hamer of the Marine Aircraft Group out of Andrews AFB," I said. "They'll be escorting you on your flight tonight."

"Very good," Kris said. He turned to the Marine pilots. "Nice birds. How fast are they?"

The first one, Kendall, spoke up. "Sir, she'll do Mach 2.25 at altitude."

A grunt that almost sounded derisive came from Blitzen. Captain Hamer looked over at the sleigh.

"Did he say something?" he asked, sounding puzzled.

Kris smiled and patted the pilot's shoulder good-naturedly.

"He just said try and keep up."

Just then, my HollyBerry buzzed in my pocket, indicating that a text message had arrived. I pulled the phone out and looked at the display. As I read the message, I smiled.

"What is it?" asked Kris.

"It's Maddox," I handed him the HollyBerry. "Your old pal from the EPA has something to tell you."

Kris took the phone from me and looked at the message:

Just letting you know everything is running great up here. Power's back on and cleanup operations are underway. How's everything there? Merry Christmas! —TM

Kris handed it back to me, laughing. "Looks like everyone's got the Christmas spirit."

I nodded. "Well," I said. "What should I tell him? How is everything here?"

Kris looked around the hangar, at the organized chaos that was unfolding, everyone running pell-mell in the service of another Christmas. Not the one any of us would have been expecting, but any Christmas, no matter how chaotic, is glorious when it's shared with the people who matter most. Kris drank it in and smiled.

"Perfect," he said, "everything is perfect."

Next came a quick rundown of the final checklist. Everything was being done on the fly here, but it was getting done, which was the most important thing. When everything seemed to be in order, he turned to me.

"Are we good?"

As I was about to answer, it seemed as though the crowd suddenly parted and in the center of the room, coming to Kris as if stepping out of a dream was Clara. The room fell silent, though the music still rang out, Judy Garland singing "Have Yourself a Merry Little Christmas," as soft and gentle as a lullaby.

She walked up to him, taking both his hands. "I had to see you off," she said.

"I wouldn't be here if it wasn't for you," he said, his face aglow.

She shook her head. "I think you would be."

"Maybe," said Kris, then looked at her face. "But I wouldn't be enjoying it half as much."

They embraced warmly as everyone whooped and applauded. Then Kris climbed up into the sleigh and grabbed the reins.

"Are you coming?" he asked, looking out into the crowd.

"Me?" I said. "No, sir! Thanks, but I've got too much to …"

Kris laughed. "Not you, Jinn." Then his eyes softened as they fell on Clara. She pressed a hand to her chest as if to confirm that she was the person he was addressing. He nodded.

"You always wanted to see London."

She didn't need any further invitation and leapt like a hurdler over the railings of the sleigh. She settled in beside him as Kris gently draped an arm over her shoulder.

"It's a bumpy ride," he teased. "Try not to fall out."

"Don't worry," she said as she rested her head on his shoulder. "I'm not going anywhere."

The reins snapped and the sleigh flew from the hanger, climbing up and up into the night. Out on the tarmac, the two Raptors rolled out and shot towards the sky in hot pursuit. The room erupted in cheers loud enough to be heard at every corner of the globe. The mayor had brought with him a few of the boys from the VFW who comprised a little Dixieland band. At once they launched into a jazzy take on "Jingle Bell Rock" and the party started in earnest. Champagne corks popped, eggnog slopped over glasses, confetti was hurled into the air. I saw a female elf dancing with an air-traffic controller, standing on his shoes like a flower girl at a wedding. Over in a corner, the mayor laughed heartily, tie loosened, his arm draped over the neck of one of the deer, who was bopping in time with the music. Harry and his family twirled around the floor, Harry's son on his shoulders, his wife laughing at his side. All was right with the world.

Amidst the celebrating, I quietly stepped away from the throng. Walking out onto the tarmac, I looked up to see the sleigh grow fainter and fainter in the distance. Seeing that dwindling shape soaring off to the sound of jingling bells on its yearly mission of peace on earth and goodwill to all, I cocked a smile and raised my glass to the sky.

"Merry Christmas, Boss."

I stood there a moment longer, watching them as they sailed away into the night, flying higher and higher until they were indistinguishable from the stars themselves.

THE END

ABOUT THE AUTHOR

Jeremy K. Brown is a writer and editor who has previously authored biographies of Stevie Wonder, Ursula K. LeGuin and Amelia Earhart. He has also written articles for various newspapers and magazines around the country. He lives in New York with his wife and family.